Proper Deafinitions

PROPER
DEAFINITIONS

collected theorograms

BETSY WARLAND

PRESS GANG PUBLISHERS

VANCOUVER

CANADIAN CATALOGUING IN PUBLICATION DATA

Warland, Betsy, 1946-
Proper deafinitions

ISBN 0-88974-021-6

1. Creation (Literary, artistic, etc.).
2. Lesbianism.   3. Feminism and literature.
I. Title.
PN56.L45W37 1990   809'.9335206643
        C90-091197-2

Some of the theorograms in *Proper Deafinitions* have been previously published. For complete publication credits see "Ways & Means,"p. 142

First Printing May 1990
1   2   3   4   5   93   92   91   90

The Publisher acknowledges financial assistance from the Canada Council.

Edited and designed by Barbara Kuhne
Typesetting and production by Val Speidel
Type produced by The Typeworks
Printed by Gagné Printing
Printed and bound in Canada

Press Gang Publishers
603 Powell Street
Vancouver, B.C.
V6A 1H2   Canada

for Daphne

Contents

Foreword

Giving *Proper Deafinitions* the slip in turns

by Louise H. Forsyth

> The brain and the womb are both centres of consciousness,
> equally important.
> (H.D., *Thought and Vision*)[1]

> Recognizing the power of the erotic within our lives can give
> us the energy to pursue genuine change within our world
> [...] For not only do we touch our most profoundly creative
> source, but we do that which is female and self-affirming in
> the face of a racist, patriarchal, and anti-erotic society.
> (Audre Lorde, "Uses of the Erotic: The Erotic as Power")[2]

> Que l'imaginaire constitue un lieu où se préserve à son meil-
> leur le code de l'espèce, cette étrange simplicité requise au
> fond pour aborder le sujet. Toute convention subjuguée, c'est
> délirant que d'approcher la matière comme une conversation
> qui dissipe l'institution.
> (Nicole Brossard, *L'amèr, ou le chapitre effrité*)[3]

In the midst of prevailing cacophony, with all its horrifying
destructive power, I feel the caress of Betsy Warland's voice
calling me, calling me urgently, across open spaces and differences, to find my own voice, to respond, to be a reader who is a
writer who is a reader who is a writer... and so will spin out
new words in new forms. Her voice celebrates in generosity and

9

with subtle humour the shimmering notion of women as seekers, as thinkers, as creators—the terrible sound and vision of women as POETS! Warland's ardent voice moves me deeply. The (f.)lips of its waves of sound hold a power much greater than this "racist, patriarchal, and anti-erotic society" has ever dared to know.

Warland's poetry and reflective texts pulse with the lucid vision and commitment of a woman who accepts no compromise in the honest expression and investigation of her passions: the body's *jouissance*, the mind's intense concentration, the anger that comes when faced with cruel, cynical and systematically perpetuated injustice. She celebrates the vitality of erotic power in her writing, an inexhaustible source of psychic, spiritual, emotional and physical energy. She does this while speaking truths that have too often stayed mysteriously unspoken in the messages that dominant discourse passes on to us. The fractured and sinuous patterns traced by her words open pregnant silences, breaks and gaps in the continuity of what is normally said. Warland and her readers stop short, recognizing patriarchy's concealed agenda, needing to choose between the easy flow of pre-packaged meaning and the challenge of playing with the enigmas of what else words and letters might be made to say, what other forms this world might dream on. At such moments, when we choose the freedom of play with her, we slip into unexpected places, places energized by forgotten memories and images which surge forth with aggressive, insistent clarity. As Nicole Brossard suggests, when we move through the looking glass of conventions pre-programmed by agents of self-interested institutions, we come to the place of our imaginary, where a strange simplicity recasts the dimensions of our subjectivity, doubling consciousness, rendering barriers fluid and porous. In this place we meet and we speak the evidence of our own truths.

The poetry of Betsy Warland's language respects this strange simplicity, enhancing its stark vigour with each new encounter, never reducing it to conventional figures of speech.

For her, language is not merely a medium. Instead, using words is a moving and creative process in a place she is currently clearing, where readers are called to participate, to join the dance. Her language is spare, elliptical, sharp, all the better to slice through empty rhetoric, dangerous taboos and concealed but effective ideological presuppositions—all the better, as well, to make a fresh start, to mark and re-mark experience on her own terms. Her writing, arising in the course of a journey into wholeness, involves desires of the body and flames of the mind, simultaneous lyric expression and theory, feeling and thinking. The processes of writing involve the playful expansion of the limits of subjective consciousness through gaps between images produced in combined imaginative and analytic reflections: "We view, we touch, this is an eye for an I—fiction/theory (tissue/text) a total body presence."[4]

Proper Deafinitions is a collection of *theorograms*—small, active and mobile texts—at work in their role as companion pieces to the narrative and lyric voices which sound in the poetry she has read and published elsewhere. What does their name mean—*theorograms*? They draw their polysemic richness from associations with *ideograms, pictograms, cryptograms,* as well as from ancient origins of the root—*gram,* suggesting writing, drawing, a letter or message, a measure of weight or sign of division. Each *theorogram* is a written shard of memory and of theory, highly condensed and suggestive, pointing to new thought, eluding precise definition, inviting each reader to come in and share its imaginative potential.

Like other Canadian and Quebec feminist writers, such as Gail Scott, Nicole Brossard, France Théoret, Louky Bersianik, Madeleine Gagnon, who have also published collections of short theoretical pieces, Warland explores some of the most problematic questions of radical feminist thought. Each piece stands on its own, suggestively evoking the vital context and intertext of feminist culture which is emerging in Canada. Each also provides other readings of Warland's own creative work, speaking the difficulties her voice has encountered as it made

11

its way on the forums of patriarchy. Warland has undertaken this reflective process as well in *Double Negative*, looking with simultaneous involvement and detachment at the poetic text as place and site where she can move outside linguistic conventions and tenacious traditions which blind. She first uses a reference to the title *Proper Deafinitions* in *Double Negative*: "here she can rest here she can play encounter her anima(l) self presign pre-time [...] words forming then shifting [...] her desire to untrain herself *undermine every prop(er) deafinition*" (my emphasis).[5] *Theorograms* would seem to be, then, short texts having a high charge of potential energy written for the purpose of transgressing and displacing a system of signs which renders dominant culture deaf to the individual's vital sound.

The texts in this book are *mind*marks of the spiralling itinerary Warland has chosen since 1983, the year in which she co-ordinated the conference *Women and Words/Les femmes et les mots*. The conference brought together about 800 women from across Canada, women who were passionately involved in writing, in thinking about writing, in understanding analytically and imaginatively how language means, works and produces values. These women wanted to see better, on the one hand, how the languages we are all conditioned to use serve to keep women on the margins of society and its cultures, and on the other hand how words are the most powerful possible instrument to move across and beyond patriarchal culture. The revolutionary impact of this conference continues to be a powerful force today for Canadian women writers. For Warland, already an active feminist writer in the 1970s, the conference marked a new turn, a coil, twist or one more dramatic spire in the spiralling path she was on. It was at this time that she brought her focus as a poet onto language, that she named the wellspring of her erotic power as lesbian, and that she saw this erotic power as the essential source of human vitality:

[...] as the writer, I affirm my sexuality, which is no longer a source of deception but a source of creativity and power.

The lesbian writer is passionate: she has risked, and will risk a great deal to love. She knows she is not alone. She believes that when you never manage to get around to reading or reviewing or teaching her books, you erase essential parts of yourself.[6]

The title of the paper she gave at the Women and Words conference, "surrendering the english language: the lesbian writer as liberator," shows the double perspective of language-focus and writing as a lesbian which has marked her work for the last seven years. In this and other early texts she expresses her despair at the dangerous uni-dimensionality of patriarchal language, as well as her astonishment at certain silences, at the absence of any expression anywhere of lesbian erotic experience.[7] Warland celebrates all manifestations of autonomous women, and so views lesbians like the virgins of which Nor Hall speaks: "belonging-to-no-man."[8] The independent, lucid, sexually aroused lesbian body does not figure at all among the images heterosexist society regularly projects for itself on its omnipresent screens of dominant culture.

Not all feminist writers agree with Warland that work on language in her poetry is the most effective way to subvert the workings of patriarchal discourse nor that it is the most dynamic means of touching the source of her own and her readers' vital energy. She has felt the chill of feminist disapproval and has hated the intolerance of difference which seemed to lie behind it. She herself makes no claims that her approach is the *right* way for all writers, but she knows it is *her* way to open a *dialogue of difference* which would interrupt, as Virginia Woolf suggested, patriarchy's processing: "if we change language / we change everything";[9] "I have no choice—this is my script: my inherited *limits, limes, borderlines between fields*. These are my de/marcations; the sites of my vision."[10]

Warland shares her passion for language-focused writing with feminists of many countries, poets like Adrienne Rich in *On Lies, Secrets, and Silence*, scholars like Dale Spender in *Man Made Language* and theologians like Mary Daly in *Gyn/Ecology* or *Wickedary*. French feminist writers have done analyses which were important to her: Simone de Beauvoir, who proclaimed in *The Second Sex* that cultural patterns are more decisive than biological factors: one is not born woman; that is what one becomes. Psychoanalyst Luce Irigaray agrees that gender conditioning is a decisive factor, but stresses the primary role played by the *sexed body*, in which is born the pulse of desire and the power of the erotic so important for Audre Lorde, for Daphne Marlatt, as well as for Betsy Warland. In her own lesbian body Warland knows the deep belly laugh so celebrated in Hélène Cixous's "Laugh of the Medusa."

The richest complicity which Warland has sustained through the period of *Proper Deafinitions* has been with feminist writers working, like her, a new synthesis of poetry and theory in periodicals such as *(f.)Lip* and *Tessera*, with lesbian writer Jane Rule following her own intense vision, and with Quebec women who feel the need to celebrate difference, displacement, deconstruction, loss and re-vision, to practice writing which produces gaps into which one risks slipping, to sweep the table clean and to set it up once again in the *desert* where women's imaginative powers, finally free of encumbering constructs, find their own fresh nourishment:

> Jane at her table (in the desert) u at your table (in the desert) Nicole at her table (in the desert) and me at this table (in the desert) not there but there writing the not here [. . .][11]

Warland works with language used lovingly, lucidly, each word carefully chosen and put in place—producing surprising images. She refuses the apparent coherence of description, regular syntax and metaphor in favour of fragmented pieces of sentences and a use of metonymy playing with centrifugal and centripetal forces, breaking and fragmenting poetic lines, leaving fissures, bringing forth traces of lost images. She plays with etymology, grammar, sounds, ellipses, repetitions, making letters and words spark with unexpected meanings as their surfaces collide. On the largely white page, silences speak with eloquence. She produces slippage of meaning through paradox as words that seem to mean one thing gracefully turn to reveal hidden facets contradicting first impressions.

The *theorograms* of *Proper Deafinitions* spiral out into broad sweeping turns, opening spaces for many women of many differences. Although speaking as a lesbian, Warland knows she does not speak for more than herself. These theoretical texts reveal, in fact, Warland's growing awareness of the complexity of feminist analysis, the impossibility of excluding from its centre analyses of racism, classism and the many other manifestations of systemic oppression. She reminds herself and her readers that white feminists are in danger of assuming white "privilege of imagination."[12]

> as a lesbian i do not speak Universese. few people do. we [. . .] come from different cultures, classes, ages, lifestyles, bodies, races, belief and educational systems. conflict in the world has been largely due to the desire "to stamp" out difference or at least have authority over it.[13]

Also integrated into the flow of these *theorograms*, creating textual counterpoint to the celebration of *jouissance* in the lesbian body, is the progressive integration of painfully suppressed autobiographical elements: incest, medical interventions, memories of silences, shame and repressed dreams learned from her mother. As Warland drafts these texts, hesitantly and with dis-ease, sets them aside, picks them up again, works further with them, integrating them into her language-focused poetics and gynogrammar, she is naming, working and carefully writing women's realities they have whispered in shame, but never dared speak publicly: " the body says 'write this.' "[14] These deceptively simple and direct texts raise questions about our own fears we do not yet dare to name, for which we still have no words, drawn from folds in the mind where the pain is most acute. The silences surrounding these folds keep us from being free.

Like Gail Scott, another language-focused Canadian writer who works in the fertile slant of exchange with Quebec feminist writers, Betsy Warland is seeking to contemplate lucidly her own painful memories, while writing into reality the intensely soft and fluid sensuality in which women's tongues, hearts and minds whirl. For both Scott and Warland, only the deconstruction of dead language forms, of their ideological underpinnings, and of all the ready-to-think clichés keeping us out of touch with our own sensuous rhythms and desires will make it possible for women to slip with our words into spaces infused with our desires.

> But the space the writing enters, attempts to decipher, is both the space of modernity (that fluid space of meaning constantly taken apart, deferred), and a space infused with our desire for a female subject-in-process. [. . .] As if a word written across a space [. . .] must immediately give way to another. So the spaces unroll around us. Like stairs . . . [15]

Sources

1. Epigraph chosen by Daphne Marlatt, *Touch to My Tongue* (Edmonton, Alta.: Longspoon Press, 1984). The field of dialogue and intertextuality opened and explored by Betsy Warland and Daphne Marlatt, each playing consecutively or concurrently reader and writer, ardent speaker and sensually responsive listener between the "scent/ences," lines and covers of their books, *open is broken*: "for Daphne" (Edmonton, Alta.: Longspoon Press, 1984) and *Touch to My Tongue*: "for Betsy," is a unique and fascinating investigation of breaking open the boundaries between texts, and so challenging traditional notions about authorship, words and discourse. Are there other examples before this in Canada where two writers, each lucidly weaving the texture of her own site of experience, explore and celebrate simultaneously the radically fresh perspective of the lesbian "sense-ability" to which each is joyously coming? The

ramifications of amorous complicity between women, when brain and womb produce elliptically mobile fields of consciousness, carry them even further in joint creations: "reading and writing between the lines" and *Double Negative*, a work juxtaposing poetic and prosaic language in the magical evocation of previously unspoken landscapes of the mind and body. (Daphne Marlatt and Betsy Warland, "reading and writing between the lines," *Tessera*, 5 (Sept. 1988), and Daphne Marlatt and Betsy Warland, *Double Negative* (Charlottetown, P.E.I.: gynergy books, 1988).

2. Audre Lorde, "Uses of the Erotic: The Erotic as Power," *Sister Outsider: Essays & Speeches* (Trumansberg, NY: The Crossing Press, 1984), 59.

3. Nicole Brossard, *L'amèr, ou le chapitre effrité* (Montréal, Que.: Quinze, 1977), 92, translated by Barbara Godard in *These Our Mothers, Or: The Disintegrating Chapter* (Toronto, Ont.: Coach House, 1983), 94.

   May the imaginary be a place where the code of the species is preserved at its best, that strange simplicity basically required to tackle the subject. All convention subjugated, it's delirious to approach matter like a conversation dispersing the institution.

4. "far as the i can see," in *Proper Deafinitions*, 79.

5. Marlatt and Warland, *Double Negative*, 51.

6. "moving parts," in *Proper Deafinitions*, 128, 136.

7. Betsy Warland, "surrendering the english language: the lesbian writer as liberator," *in the feminine* (the conference proceedings), edited by Ann Dybikowski, Victoria Freeman, Daphne Marlatt, Barbara Pulling & Betsy Warland (Edmonton, Alta.: Longspoon Press, 1985) and Betsy Warland, "untying the tongue," *open is broken* (Edmonton, Alta.: Longspoon Press, 1984).

8. "far as the i can see," in *Proper Deafinitions*, 77.

9. "the breasts refuse," in *Proper Deafinitions*, 25.

10. "suffixscript," in *Proper Deafinitions*, 37.

11. Marlatt and Warland, *Double Negative*, 54.

12. "the white page," in *Proper Deafinitions*, 62.

13. "up-ending universality," in *Proper Deafinitions*, 59.

14. "cutting re/marks," in *Proper Deafinitions*, 103.

15. Gail Scott, *Spaces like Stairs* (Toronto, Ont.: The Women's Press, 1989), 11-12.

the breasts refuse

As a girl-child, i learned that women's words were applied like cosmetics; learned that we were necessarily deceptive—to protect and make presentable the vulnerable face of our inadequate gender.

As an adolescent, i heard a Black Civil Rights leader reveal the encoded racism within our words. He spoke of "little white lies" and "evil black lies." He gave many examples. My remaining innocence about language ended that day.

During university and Vietnam, i witnessed the co-opting of Peace Movement language: "Peace in Our Time," and "Peace Initiatives"; Nixon's smile and the acquiescence to the leadership of lies.

Feminism filled in the blank; began a new vocabulary. "Girl," "chick," "patriarchy," and "sexist:" we would never again accept "it's just a word!"

In France and Quebec, feminists deconstructed sexism within the grammatical structure of French. Playing with words, coining new ones, creating a feminist curren(t)cy—we began to cross each other's borders sans passport: to sense a new country of minds.

Black feminist writers in the U.S. were breaking the stranglehold of White English grammar. In English Canada, we increasingly felt compelled to investigate our own "invisible oppression" within language. Daly and Spender also crossed our borders, crossed our minds.

In my early 30s, i reached a crisis with language. In relocating my writing within my lesbian body, i found that language, by omission and negative connotation, had denied the intimate world of my eroticism and love. Brossard, Rich, Lorde, Cixous, and Irigaray broke sexual taboos, and i dis-covered my words; marked the page; have never been the same.

It is interesting to note that most of the language-focused feminist writers in English Canada come to the English language at a slant: either because this is our second language or culture, or because we come from different races. Perhaps it is the cumulative effects of these various dislocations which provoke what has been called our "obsession with language."

I
breaking the patriarchal headlock

1955
the Saturday Night Wrestling Match
my brothers and me
in front of the t.v.
yelling for our favourite wrestler to win
he puts a headlock on his opponent
the guy is rendered helpless
looks ridiculous
huge man being led around the ring
it's not a winning hold
it's a hold for belittling the ego
provoking the crowd's jeers
imposing an isolating passivity
in the midst of public action

head, kaput, corporal, cattle, capital, chief, cape
the *head*?
    it's *kaput,*
être capot, to have lost all tricks at cards,
be hoodwinked, from capot, cloak with hood, from cape

a cloak-and-dagger language

Webster's Condensed Dictionary of the English Language
Twentieth Century Edition (1906)
establishing the correct
spelling, pronunciation, and definitions of words
based on
The Unabridged Dictionary of Noah Webster

same black bumpy-leather cover
as The Bible
pages edged with red
not of her curse
but of his victory

Noah setting his dicktionary afloat
on the sons (painting the town red)
& daughters (in the red)
of the New World

keeping his head
above water
language the mimesis of his value system

II
proper deafinitions

"Make all the sentences in a paragraph 'hang together,' make

each sentence grow out of what preceded and leads naturally to
what follows; and so arrange the sentences that it is impossible
to change their order without a loss of clearness."

sentence, sentire, to feel
over & over she's caught red-handed
feeling her way
with her own
sense, sent-, sentence
her own
language, lingua, tongue

                                      red rag to a bull

he belittles "on the rag?"
he castigates "rag, rag!"

she sees red

then later
dis-covers
red rag is
"Old slang for tongue"
and his mean-ing
is changed

she puts on some ragtime
smiles dancing on her face

                                            red tape

his word is law
(*archaic, "to bullyrag"*)

her monthly red-handedness
her tongue's teleology

language, he maintains, is neuter

she looks it up—
neuter, ne-, no + uter, either (see ne, see kwo-),
ne- no, deny + kwo-, alibi
language *no alibi!*
she muses on his red herring
as language becomes
new-to-her

". . . the masculine is not the masculine but the general."

general, gene-; gender, degenerate, genius, indigen, germinate,
genesis, pregnant, nature, cognate, Kriss Kringle, kin, genus,
genitor, heterogeneous, gent, germ, genitalia, genocide

just call him Gene!
that pretty much sums it up

the Universal He (for general usage)
unable to tolerate
being referred to by
the Universal She

                                        red light

". . . there are 220 words for a sexually promiscuous female
and only 20 for a sexually promiscuous male."

laws can be changed
but if language remains the same
the repressed returns
in a word
barely missing a step

"Do not omit the subject of the sentence."

our mother's advice
give him his head
gender lineage of
"minus male" & "negative semantic space"
head over heels in love with his manologues

PRACTICE: Sit before the mirror with chin in hand
and rehearse the look of fascination in your eyes.
Nod and smile repeatedly, murmuring "How
interesting."

". . . 98% of interruptions in mixed conversations
were made by males."

the most frequently cited (77%) cause of women's anger:
"He doesn't listen to me."

language is a value system
bringing us to the edge of global destruction
a system of polarities
(man/woman, good/evil, light/dark)
which eradicate the intricate and complex differences
of minus male
and minus white
peoples & cultures

"Avoid constructions and statements that admit of a double
meaning."

red line

don't cross over it
the feminine's absence so familiar
so profound
even women's organizations have been known
to reject inclusive terms

disdain non-gendered words

        1) denial & isolation
        2) anger
        3) bargaining
        4) depression
        5) acceptance

        the attitude toward
        our changing language
        somewhere between
        stages 1) & 2) of dying

language of the mass media
depleted, deceptive

if we change language
we change everything

if we continue to accept language as a
given, ghabh-, malady
we must ask ourselves
are we then accomplices
of our White Fathers' Monopoly Game To End All Monopoly
    Games
our White Fathers' Master Race/Space Plan
our White Fathers' Big Bang

                    malady

m'lady?
damsels in des-
truction
or
decoders
X-posers

of subtextual brainwashing
in words like "bloodbath"
           "massacre"
           "meltdown"
routinely used
in reference to
the stock-market collapse
of October 1987

                              BREAK THE HEADLOCK!

wrestle your way out of passivity
through deconstruction
           word play
           etymology
           invention
through colloquial contextualizing

feel, sentire, sentence
the elation of
your *existence, ex-, out + sisere, to take a position, stand firm*
on the page
be *responsible, respondere, to respond*
to your own red rags

                                        red flag

the Fathers will say "it's awkward"
                    "it's sexist"
                    "it doesn't sound right"
                    "it's racist"
                    "it's not proper grammar"

and we'll laugh our
heads off
put down the looking glass

as our *smile* becomes our *smei-, mirror*
recalling how they said this about Black writers
(rag-tag "the rabble, the 'Great Unwashed' ")
said "this isn't literature"
    "these people don't know how to write"

but they wrote on
grabbed the tagrag
and ran off at the mouth
made themselves present
in the language
in our living-rooms
let their words go to their heads
let their words be red

language, dnghu, bilingual
not masculine or feminine
as i first had thought
but the language
which has been allowed
and the language
which has not

i no longer seek a language which is in opposition to
which would yet again obliterate difference

there are only dialects
our project:
to write our own

                                        a red letter day

when i take my oral language
and translate it into
new-to-her forms

"Do not use in serious writing words and expressions that are
allowable only in familiar conversations."

ignore Gene's red neck!
unstop every proper deafinition
question every word
investigate every letter
dis-cover every grammatical rule

rag "from Old Norse rogg, tuft"
tuft "a short cluster of yarn, hair . . .
        attached at the base or growing
        close together . . . see tap-,
                                tampon"

take the red marking pen
and write with it
your dialect "A variety of language that,
                with other varieties,
                constitutes a single language,
                of which no single variety is standard."

i believe our survival depends on it

III
the breasts refuse

the danger of dialects

divisive
disruptive
difficult to control

historically having been
either gradually absorbed into one dominant language

or
splintering off into
independent "foreign" languages

are there other options?

rethinking the Tower of Babel
variations on this myth found around the world
God's anger striking down the heaven-reaching tower,
ziggurat, man-made mountain, pyramid, or great tree
                                        confusion of tongues
the punishment
or
was it an act of liberation from
the tyranny of one language?

ego-centrism of erections
enslaving difference to
its *monument, men-, mind, mania, money, muse, amnesia*

stone by
            stone

God's anger at their arrogance
or was it rage
at these ruling men's cruelty?

street car in Toronto
white man yelling at two Italian women who speak animatedly
"God-damned immigrants, speak CANADIAN, eh?"

mother tongue
oral   original   open
mnemonic   repetitious   clichéd
spiralling   sound   integrative
concrete, com-, together + crescere, to grow

domestic   ecological
presence and involvement of
both speaker and listener

father language
written   learned   closed
dissembling   differentiating   sequential
linear   sight   exclusive
abstract, ab-, away + trahere, to pull
absence and unequal involvement of
writer and reader

"With writing, the earlier noetic state [primary orality]
undergoes a kind of cleavage, separating the knower from the
external universe and then from himself."

separation of the knower from the known
knowledge as background
man as foreground
focal point in the picture
"knowledge-by-analysis"
replacing "knowledge-by-empathy"

and along with it
the development of written languages
for and by men

languages alienated from the daily domestic life
not of the mother
but of the father
exclusive ruling class languages
for privileged, professional men
Sanskrit, Classical Chinese, Classical Arabic, Rabbinic Hebrew
the "linguistic economies"
which constructed our thought world

and so we must ask
what is the relationship between
the instinct which created
a written language
for recording material surplus and exchange
and the instinct which created
capitalism?

now
capitalism totters
language is being deconstructed
genres blur
science concedes its nonobjectivity
ecology forces us to acknowledge our interrelatedness
and the oppressed refuse their stoney silence

cracks in these "sacred"
closed systems of thought
heard around the world

"The tendency to closure had to do with a state of mind
encouraged by print and its way of suggesting that knowledge,
and thus indirectly actuality itself, could somehow be pack-
aged."

the walls of the Fathers'
exclusive, ex-, out + claudere, to shut
classical languages
crumbling

Latin falling into gradual disuse
with the admission of girls and women
into academia

current writing theories & practices
beginning to recognize and invite

readers to re-enter the text

the reader grows up
is interested in other options

dawn of the "neo-oral?"

there is a danger
in replacing language dominance
with the illusion of language accessibility
a danger in
convincing ourselves that the
"mass languages with megavocabularies"
(such as English & Mandarin)
are the
new "living mother tongues"
and yet again
dismiss the power of language
as an encoded value system

Babel reinscribed
on a pseudo breast as phallus

throw down your stones!

the breasts refuse
inherently know
the presence of the other
even in their pairs
differ greatly

NO MORE MONUMENTS!

in my writing
i seek a dialect
an *intercourse, intercurrere, to run between* the oral and the

written
a provocative relationship
where neither accepts the other
at face value

i am both mother and father
and i am neither

you may or may not understand my dialect
i may or may not understand yours
in this, at the very least,
we admit
how little understanding has been exchanged
when difference is denied
by the illusion
of a shared language

in naming our selves
we finally accept
our babbles' necessity

Sources

The American Heritage Dictionary of the English Language (Boston: Houghton Mifflin Company, 1969).

The Rev. E. Cobham Brewer, *The Brewer Dictionary of Phrases and Fable*, (originally published in 1870), (Hertfordshire, UK: Mega Books, 1986).

Shere Hite, *Women and Love* (New York: Random House, 1987).

Walter J. Ong, *Interfaces of the Word* (Ithaca, NY: Cornell University Press, 1977).

Walter J. Ong, *Fighting for Life* (Ithaca, NY: Cornell University Press, 1981).

Dale Spender, *Man Made Language* (London: Routledge and Kegan Paul, 1980).

George B. Woods, and Clarence Stratton, *A Manual of English* (Garden City, NY: Doubleday, Page and Company, 1926).

"minus male," Geoffrey Leech, cited in Casey Miller and Kate Swift, *Words and Women* (Garden City, NY: Anchor Press, 1976).

"negative semantic space," Julia Penelope Stanley, cited in *Words and Women* (Garden City, NY: Anchor Press, 1976).

suffixscript

It is just over a year since I finished writing "the breasts refuse." At that point I was very aware of the impact of socialization, homophobia, and the civil rights movement on my experience of the English language. In the interim, I have finally come to grips with two other crucial influences: my recovery of incest memories, and my speaking English as if it were my second language.

(m.) Brain wave? As an incest victim of familial male sexual abuse, I watched how my abusers conceived and rationalized their violation and manipulation of my body by making language into a vehicle for deception and denial. (m.) Brain wash: CONsequently, I experienced the abusers' power of words to not only erase but to cruelly invert the truth. (f.) Brain waive—I absorbed my abusers' words of blame and denial, which obliterated my own words of fear and pain.

Although I grew up speaking English, I learned it within the environment of a Norwegian rural community and family who spoke it as their second language. We were the first generation not allowed to learn Norwegian, yet adult emotional conversations occurred in Norwegian, much to our fascination and frustration. As a result, Norwegian syntax and sentence structure form an invisible grid on my mind and English will never have the ease and gut-feeling of a mother tongue.

As writers, particularly as women writers, we are compelled to question the nature of our relationship to the English language. Examine it much as a visual artist must scrutinize a material medium. The method and intensity with which each woman writer pursues this *investigation (in-, + vestigare, to trace, track, from trace, footprint*) is idiosyncratic and entirely self-determined. I have chosen to foreground this process because of my various language/life experiences. As a writer, I have found this process to be a source of exhiliration and endless creative possibilities. This foregrounding, which is done in various ways by a number of women writers across Canada and Quebec, is frequently interpreted not as a personal choice but as a prescriptive dictate for others. This reaction, which is often dismissive and hostile, is particularly associated with other women writers who believe the English language and grammar to be neutral in terms of an encoded value system. So, among us women writers who are feminists, there is considerable disagreement about the nature of the language we work within.

Among those of us who are practicing language-focused or language-centred writing, can a delineation be made between women writers and men writers? For me, there is a crucial dissimilarity located in the driving *motive, mew-, emotion*. For the woman writer, it is a matter of necessity and survival: for herself; for the women (and men) her work resonates with; and ultimately, for the species. For the man writer, it is often a matter of game and innovation. There are exceptions—particularly men writers of colour who are (along with women writers of colour) transcribing their oral, culture-specific dialect of English onto the page.

Much of language-centred white men writers' work is fueled by an understandable despair and cynicism about Western/urban/mass media culture and politics. The absence in their visions of a *radical, radix, root* analysis of the patriarchy, however, all too frequently generates writing which is aggressive, cynical, or enervated, resulting in writing which is actually complicit with the very culture (and language) they seem to critique.

One of the men writers who is an exception to this generalization is bp Nichol. Nichol's playfulness with language freed him to slip out the side door of proper grammar and proper male behaviour. His playfulness enabled him to critique gently and, perhaps most importantly (and in this he was unusual among men writers), to circumvent the despair of the dominator's role: it enabled him to delight in the daily world as a co-inhabitant.

Sometimes I say, "Why make it so difficult for yourself, Betsy? You're already up against it as a woman writer who is not only a feminist, but a lesbian as well—why be a language-focused writer too?" Let's face it: this isn't a very smart approach if you'd like to reach a larger audience—which every writer longs to do.

I have no choice—this is my script: my inherited *limits, limes, borderlines between fields*. These are my de/marcations; the sites of my vision.

mOther muse:/«mousa, mosaic»

how do i (w)right you
you i have protected myself from
for so long
even in my crib
listened intently
how you moved from room to room
not wanting to agitate turn turn tension tighter
you were my mOther
so foreign māter-: «matter»
though the world said the opposite
in every book & greeting card
that we were intimates
in( )mates
crying in the basement
dark walls of depression
closing in after i was born
snowless black fields surrounding
your story of how thrilled you were that i was a girl
always about my father's beaming face brown tie
    (which you still recall)
as he leaned over and kissed you
where were you you do not speak of yourself
only the cold metal-table covered with other women's blood
six births before me so fast no time to clean up
and me a breech each
year you recount beaming face tie kiss
words as erasure
it was you who taught me to distrust
their surface
you on the telephone like in front of a mirror
applying them again and again to your offspring's images

makeup madeup altered conversations and events only
hours old
i barely recognized myself
cosmetology of your words for the Others' gaze/appraise
and everyone was the Other (including yourself)
we were strangers from the beginning
tormented by our difference
which did not exist

M: «Around 1000 B.C. the Phoenicians and other Semites and
Palestines began to use a graphic sign representing the consonant *m* . . . they named the sign mēm, meaning
"*water*" . . . »

O: «. . . they gave it the name cayin, meaning "*eye*" . . . »

D: «. . . dāleth, meaning "*door*" . . . »

E: «. . . hē and used the consonant *h* . . . »

waiting at the door
entering

R: «. . . resh, meaning "*head*" . . . »

crowning
emerging
her door opens wide
MODER?

40

no,

MOTHER.

«As in the case of Father, the substitution of the *th* for the earlier *d* dates from the beginning of the sixteenth c.»

and what was lost with the *d*?

D: «Corresponding letters—Sanskrit dwr, Celtic duir, Hebrew
   dāleth,—meant the Door of birth, death, or sexual
   paradise... in India it was Yoni Yantre, or yantra of the
   vulva.»

«d»

sensation of

coming up through the earth

self-possession

«th»

sensation of fragility

energy going out from the mouth   hanging in air

waiting for someone to take it

41

my mOther calls me

through the dusk «youuu-whooo—Betsy—youuu-whooo . . . »

her "you-who" surfs airwaves

my name a slur in comparison

this ōō-ōō irritates & intrigues

one word two syllables   you/affirmation & who/doubt

intimacy & strangeness

rising settling
                in a single held moment

her daughter   out there   somewhere

in the barn the woods on her horse in the fields

my voice returns

through divide of night & day
                                «cooomiiing»

shared eroticism of absence

repression the uncut cord between us

i never touched myself never even thought of it

just like the movies

your twin beds

both feet on the floor at all times

did she ever come? (we ask)

the question hooks off

period of certainty

she had *kids* didn't she

                                        question mark
                                        half a bleeding heart

                                        ?

Renaissance «re-, again +
                              nascī, to be born»

change from agriculture-based economy

to commercial and capitalist society

manufacturing arms and moveable field artillery

printing the first book—the Gutenberg Bible

burning Joan of Arc

uprising of peasants

expelling Jews from country after country

Luther and Calvin

first circumnavigation of the globe

and Man's discovery of spermatozoon in the microscope

the Fathers' desire—all that virgin land

and with His new found virility

the «d» was replaced

He had the world to invent «in-, on +
                                        venīre, to come»

Mother stayed home

in a house without door

mmmOther
thirty years later

in another country
i hear "youuu-whooos"

in harbour fog horn

& airplane service-call tones

same reversed musical third
of your call-
                    ing

daughter of "you-who"

left

to come

calling no

daughter in the dark

no central character

Memory, goes back to the Indo-European root *smer-*, which the word *mourn* is also derived from.

This is about memory. A kind of memory that a great many of us have fiercely repressed. A kind of memory which we have no awareness of. Which profoundly shapes our intimate lives without our understanding. Without our assent. It has no relationship to formal education or "remember when . . . " This memory is the interface (inner face) of a self-induced amnesia. Sometimes it occurs when, as adults, we suffer some horrific event alone. More frequently, it occurs when, as children, we suffer a deeply disillusioning event alone. It has to do with being victimized, usually an invisible victimization. No witnesses. "No visible scars."[1]

So why seek out this memory? Why not leave "well enough" alone? So, you've happened to build your house on top of a toxic waste deposit: just don't dig around, stir things up, or plant a garden. Sell and don't tell. Not possible.

A brief bio. I spent the first thirty years of my life with practically no sexual sensations or feelings. Certainly no orgasms. No self-exploration or self-stimulation. Yet I was a very passionate person. Deeply involved in all other facets of my life. After an eight year marriage, I felt compelled to determine if, in fact, I was a lesbian. The marriage ended. I did fall in love with a woman. We were lovers for four years. My sexual, sensual self became very much alive. I concluded that my repressed lesbianism had kept my sexual self in deep freeze for all those years. Yet there were problems with this new sexual intimacy

47

too. Eventually, my lover "betrayed me" by having an affair. I fell into a profound depression, experienced a primary sense of abandonment. Realized that I had been terrified of this happening my whole life. Wondered why. Moved away and began my life over. But just before my departure, I happened to see a video. A video I attended only as a gesture of support for a friend who had arranged its public screening. It was comprised of six incest survivors talking to one another about their processes of coming to terms with their incest. By the end of the screening, I knew this video had something to do with me. I knew it clearly, but had no idea as to how or who or when.

The next four years I spent reading, talking to incest survivors, looking over childhood family photographs, and asking my one sibling I'm close to (who has a good memory) about the sexual dynamics that were operating in our extended family. The tracks had been well covered by us all, but there were pieces of the story here and there. Only fragments. During these years the backdrop filled itself in. No plot. No central characters. Then came the shock of another family member who, under great distress during a familial crisis, admitted to being a victim of incest. Suddenly, this family member's chronic and maddening fear of being taken advantage of made sense! The hiding of valuables and then the accusing others of stealing them; the resentments so deeply held.

You are probably aware by now of my use of non-specific nouns for my family. I still feel compelled to protect them as individuals. They are caught in the net-of-never-tell. Only I have decided to write this.

With this revelation of incest, I finally had evidence. Affirmation that I hadn't been imagining things. Incest did exist within our extended family. This was the point at which I began to work with Cheryl, a feminist therapist. Though I had only a brief period of time before I moved back to Vancouver, I knew I was ready. Ready somehow to unearth my own memories. Fortunately, Cheryl recognized this, and agreed to fit me in on a short-term basis. We had seven sessions. She suggested that she teach me self-hypnosis. Since I sensed that this might be the only way in, I agreed. There was a practicality about this approach and about Cheryl's presence which I found reassuring. Through self-hypnosis, I regained my ability to establish my inner place of safety. The very place, I suspect, that was trespassed and violated in me as a child.

In the second session, my first memory reconstructed itself. I say "reconstructed itself" because it seemed like that. It initially felt like a very bizarre process. I trusted it, however, because I felt safe, essentially in control, and I had a reliable witness. My body led the way. Chest tightening with panic as I fell backward in time. Everything was black. Like a movie theatre with all the lights out. I think now, that terrible nothingness was the thick membrane of amnesia I had to pass through. The first fragment surfaced on my mind-screen; the word "hotel." What did that mean? Lights out again. It seemed so bizarre. Cheryl urged me to keep trusting myself. And I sat in the nothingness and waited. Then the scene of the upstairs of our house flashed in front of me. Where our family bedrooms were. Lights out again. Chest painful from constriction. And so it went. This jerky motion like an old silent film which kept stopping and starting, skipping numerous frames but somehow allowing the central images of the story to appear. When it was over, I said what all incest victims say, "I must have made it up." Cheryl responded, "Why would you do that?" We talked. Through the talking I began to accept this unfamiliar memory process, the way these bizarre pieces string themselves together even though they seem, at first, to make no sense.

During our last sessions, we spent most of the time exploring the impact of my reconstructed memory and discussed what I needed to do to continue my healing process. The most valuable comment Cheryl made to me was that incest doesn't come out of the air: it is a learned behaviour and the family member who victimized me was very likely victimized by someone else first. This insight was critical in focusing my attention and anger on the dynamics of my extended family instead of simply singling out another one of its victims.

I now believe that both people are victimized by incest. The nature of the victimization is different, however. The one who is taken advantage of is left considerably more powerless and more terrorized. I still rage at the prevalence of this invisible brainwashing of young girls. See rape as a "refresher course" which reminds women to always wear this fear of unprovoked attacks like chains around our necks. This is a method of enslavement. But the *perpetrators, perpetrāre, "to perform in the capacity of the father,"* suffer damage too. I cannot speak for them. Only know that they must work to heal themselves, as well.

As well. Well. Memory is like a . . . ; yes, I am . . . , thank you. More accurately, I am getting there. Two years after working with Cheryl, I wrote my perpetrator. It was a confronting letter about our incest, our family's pattern; but it was also a letter which was written with love and concern. In my letter, I urged this family member to begin to work toward personal healing. If incest is to stop, everyone must take responsibility for healing themselves. In response to my letter, this family member accepted the premise of my confrontation but admitted to having no memory of it. True regret was expressed as well as the assurance that "I will undoubtedly keep thinking about this for a long time to come." It takes a long time. It has now been six and a half years for me. Seven years is said to be the average length of recovery time.

Since those sessions with Cheryl, other memories have surfaced periodically. Finally, I knew how to recognize them. Some came through hypnosis, others through dreams or associative experiences. The plot and characters gradually filled themselves in. Although some incest survivors do vividly recall their experiences, most of us don't. With Cheryl, I understood that the recovery of my experience was never going to come back as a whole, intact memory.

The imprint of unresolved incest on our adult lives is very real, very tangible. Tangible, once you learn to recognize its shape; sense its presence; remember its gestures—you catch yourself incest-shadowing current associative dynamics with your intimates. This shadowing is very subtle and very subversive. This is why it is imperative that we do "dig around." But first, establish a safe place. Find someone who has experience with incest survivors, who has the skills to work with your amnesia. A counsellor or therapist who knows how to witness; who recognizes your reconstructing fragments. Include your intimates in your process, because your healing has repercussions on them.

My repressed lesbianism is not what froze my sexuality for thirty years. In talking with other lesbians, I grew to realize that nearly all of them knew an active sexuality within themselves (fantasy and self-stimulation) and with others (female and/or male) before they came to terms with their lesbianism. No, it was the freezer door of incest that had slammed tight. It has taken me perhaps half of my life to pry it open again. I write this with the hope that it won't take so long for you.

Sources

1. Angela Hryniuk, "mirror window drawer," unpublished poem.

f.) is sure

I'm going to play around in my talk with the title of our panel, "Across the Cultural Gap,"[1] and look at some related clichés and sayings. *To blow the gap*, give information. Gap: an opening; a fissure; a break or pass through the mountains; a suspension of continuity; a conspicuous difference; a space traversed by an electrical spark; from Old Norse, chasm; to open the mouth, yawn. I love how etymologies always seem to take us back to the mouth! So, here we are, talking about the mouth again. Yes, I have to wonder what the "yawn" is about and I suspect what it calls up is how we deal with difference among ourselves. After we've first encountered difference and recovered from the initial terror, I think that what we often do is quickly move into a stance of saying, oh it's boring to talk about this again; it's wearing; it's a drag; let's talk about something interesting—which is usually yet another topic about ourselves.

So, across the cultural mouth. It is a cross we bear, this supposed collective mouth we're repeatedly told represents us all. We know who makes it through the "opening," who "pass"(es), which rhymes with blast—we know who has the dynamite power in the mountains of our collective teeth. We know who has the electrically amplified voices. Those of us here are whispers in this collective head. We're the voices that make the jaw clench.

To stop two gaps with one bush. This is an Old English saying which is actually another version of "to kill two birds with one stone." More and more has been written about feminine writing in the fissure—a writing which is attempting to no longer beat around the bush, around some topics, and we're becoming—think of the word "fissure,"—(f.), for the feminine gender, is

53

sure! That's what's beginning to happen I think with some of these voices. It's no coincidence that most of the language-focused and language-concerned women writers who are feminists in English Canada come to the English language at a slant, to use a phrase of Emily Dickinson's. This is often because we're writing from a second language or culture and/or race. For some of us, the disparity is not obvious. For instance, I'm a blond, blue-eyed, middle-class, white, stereotype western woman. I'm the image that is invariably trotted out to make the points about racism and sexism.

To stop the gap, secure a weak point; prevent attack. When I was thirty years old I finally realized that I speak English as a second language—this is not metaphorically speaking—this is actually true. It's not a coincidence that I realized this during the same period of time that I came out as a lesbian because it was, in fact, my first woman lover who pointed this out to me. It made sense, finally, of why I always have difficulty with grammar and sentence structure. I seldom construct a sentence in the way that I should—at least in the beginning. It also made sense of why it's so difficult for me to speak in public without notes or a written text that I can rework and revise (which I do a lot of) ahead of time. And even when I'm on a one-to-one basis and I'm really involved in an intense conversation around ideas (I'm ok with emotions), but with ideas—the words just blow away: gone! I spend half my brain time trying to catch them again. The reason is because I grew up in a Norwegian, rural community. My grandparents all came from Norway; that whole generation came from Norway. My parents were the first generation to grow up speaking both languages and my generation was the first to speak English as our mother tongue. But I was learning English from people who were all speaking it as a second language. They were trying valiantly to imitate what they thought was proper English. This was in the U.S. and there was a tremendous pressure. You felt compelled to be a part of the melting pot; to fit in, to "pass." On top of this, all the important adult conversations occurred in Norwegian but we were not allowed to learn Norwegian, so there was a real double message there. So, it's like I have this invisible pattern of the Norwegian language implanted on my brain yet I don't even know the language.

Next, in terms of language, came my experience as an incest victim. I learned very profoundly that language is not to be trusted. It is all too often a vehicle for deception. If I stated my reality, it was totally denied, so my choice was to withdraw into myself. My silence was all I had to protect me from losing myself and my reality. It was the only way I could keep clear about what was really going on. It took me 34 years to even begin to remember this: that's how severe the repression of this painful experience was. My first memory came back to me with a single word echoing in my head, the word "hotel." No, it wasn't "just a game."

To open the gap, give access to. More recently, my experience as a lesbian and its impact on my sense and use of the English language has affected me as a writer. In my first book, *A Gathering Instinct* (which came out in 1981), the last three poems in that book were the first poems I wrote as a lesbian. They were love poems and they were intentionally non-gendered, universal love poems—so you couldn't really tell anything about the gender of either lover. This was intentional because I was afraid. Later, as I became more grounded in my life as a lesbian, and my vision as a lesbian, I came smack up against the reality that there were no words for my experience—my erotic, sexual and spiritual experiences as a lesbian. In my second book, *open is broken* (which came out in 1984), I started to sink myself into language; I began to take it apart and make up words and reclaim it. That's when I came into a deep realization that language is a value system. It's not neutral. It's a value system created and maintained by patriarchal, white, middle-class, heterosexual, educated people who generally tyrannize the rest

of the world. My understanding of this language/power structure has profoundly shaped my work ever since.

To stand in the gap, act as defender. Those of us working with
language, and consequently form (often the two go together),
are increasingly being criticized. I was actually surprised when
Viola[2] commented on that. But it's true. And, in fact, there's been
hostility lately. This often comes from other women writers,
many of them feminists, who say things like "leave the language
alone; it's perfectly adequate—you're just covering up bad writing." [laughter from audience and panel]. Sounds familiar? Many
of them say that the tradition and the mainstream present no
problems for them as women writers. I'm not necssarily in argument with their experiences, but I am in argument with their
criticisms, because we are told that our writing is negative,
narrow, patriarchy-bashing, and that it's for "card carrying
members." In fact, those of us involved in experimenting with
language in English Canada—well, our relationships are very er-
ratic; some of us rarely even talk to each other. Most of us don't
really know each other very well—so this last criticism is pretty
bizarre. A criticism which came up recently in an interview with
several B.C. women writers was that there's only one person to
do this, "and everybody else is just like a cookie cutter."[3] This
"one person" is Nicole Brossard, whose work I greatly admire.
But to me this judgement smells of tokenism—like there can
only be one lesbian writer who can do language-focused writing. In fact, a lot of the language-focused writers in English Canada aren't lesbian or white, but this doesn't matter, right? We all
sort of look alike: you can't really tell the difference—there's
only one that's authentic. Which probably translates into the
mainstream only wanting to deal with one: one's enough! What
all this is about is fear. Fear blurs our vision. When we are
afraid, we cannot perceive the specifics of difference. We can
only perceive our fear.

The criticism I feel the most angry about is when I hear that feminist language-focused writers are being "prescriptive," even, it's been said (in the same interview), "morally prescriptive." This is The Great Reversal! This is a strategy from the patriarchy—where you turn things around and accuse others of the very thing you're doing. The tradition in the mainstream is to assert (and believe) that art is not prescriptive or political. The norm is not political, right? It's just the norm. But they say to writers who are working outside the mainstream that our writing is political; that our writing isn't really literature. This goes for women writers of colour, lesbian-feminist writers, language-focused writers, whatever. And I'm saying that we must not be intimidated and silenced by these criticisms, even when they come from women who are friends and acquaintances, even when we feel betrayed, even when it hurts like hell.

A cultured mouth. Culture, Latin, cultura, cultivate, to loosen the earth around plants to destroy the weeds. Point of view: who are the plants and who are the weeds? Point of vision: why don't we all be weeds? Now that's when writing gets interesting, you know. We need all the dialects, *to fill in the gap*, make up a deficiency, fill in a vacant space. Because we are absent in the English language as women who are self-defined and named. So, we're free to invent, reclaim, redis-cover language on a word-to-word basis: like children—the power, the sensuousness and the magic of words. This is where language becomes very spiritual for me; when it is not a given but a gift.

Sources

1. Simon Fraser University Women's Studies conference, *Telling It: Women and Language Across Cultures* (Vancouver, November 1988).

2. Viola Thomas, moderator of the panel discussions at the conference *Telling It: Women and Language Across Cultures*.

3. "Getting into Heaven: An Interview with Diana Hartog, Paulette Jiles, and Sharon Thesen," *The Malahat Review* 83 (Summer 1988).

up-ending universality

as a writer, what is my relationship to LITERATURE: "deph-, To stamp" (of approval)? does writing out of my lesbian body speak the words of the Universal Mouth? to the Universal Ears? is this not the MARK: "mearc, boundary, landmark, sign" of the Universal Voice? as a lesbian i do not speak Universese. few people do. we (collective not universal) come from different cultures, classes, ages, lifestyles, bodies, races, belief and educational systems. conflict in the world has been largely due to the desire "to stamp" out difference or at least have authority over it ("everything's under control"). "universal" comes from the same Indo-European root as the word "versatile." Judy Grahn speaks of "multi-versality" in contrast to universality. what we write inevitably excludes most people. yet if we write well we invite eavesdropping by the other and with INTEREST: "interesse, 'to be in between' " s/he hears the difference of an/other's life. it is *in* difference we understand our own lives more profoundly. our child-learned fear of being excluded, "left out" programs us to grow up into the adult enforcers of mandatory homogeneity and heterogeneity. most often when we encounter exclusion we are fearful or indignant, not intrigued. perhaps this is because of the "fixed" roles of who has the power to exclude and who does not. the language itself controls us. a language formed prior to the theory of relativity. if we "move away" from our original community, we are often told upon return visits "you haven't changed a bit; you're just the same." as children we are taught a communal set of clichés which describe our encounters with others. these clichés define the parameters of *how* we experience difference. if we define experience outside these clichés—we become "outsiders." most of us then leave, to begin the life-long process of "writing home." our homing instinct our own words. language-centred writing is a writing which embraces relativity. the roles break down. it brings *out* the "left out"; reveals the multi-versality of a word. in my own writing i dis/cover relativity through etymology, deconstructing clichés & symbols and juxtaposing quotes from disparate sources. in my first years of writing i attempted to find relativity through the use of metaphor. this writing, however, is actually based on similarity: its urge is to belong. ("you're just the same.") in my thirties i became increasingly aware of my difference and the necessity for my writing to embody this. i had written myself into a corner with metaphors and my difference was suffocating. as sense of my body TISSUE: "teks-, text" changed so did sense of my text. in Literature much has been "left out" about all of our lives. it is the "left out" which interests us most: we have the greatest need to know. the things your mother never told you. i believe writing we value is writing which springs from necessity. the necessity to speak the unspoken, the taboo of our lives. if we do not, we BETRAY: "trans-, over + dare, to give" ourselves over, turn ourselves in, become agents of our own absence. my writing does not TRANSCEND: "trans-, over + scandere, to climb" (over what/who?) i write to "change the textual reality within which it is inscribed" (Monique Wittig). in the beginning was the WER-: "Base of various Indo-European roots; to turn, bend. Universe, versatile, verse, version, transverse" pre-Copernicus thinking and Adam's Garden Grammar forged the Universal He with the rest of us (women, children and less privileged men) revolving around his HE-liocentric son. in my writing i turn from the Universal toword a transversal voice.

the white page

You're a white feminist writer. You have just encountered a deeply felt and clearly stated directive from your sister writers of colour to desist from writing out of their cultures. What do you do? What if you are against censorship (which I am); how do you reconcile your belief in freedom of speech with this directive? Are they the same, or are they different? I, like many feminist artists, have not come to my position of anti-censorship easily, but I have come to realize that in asserting my right to write openly as a feminist lesbian, I must also accept the pornographer's right. For ultimately, no governing body within the patriarchy could ever be trusted to understand the difference between the two.

So what do you do if you've just finished a novel you've been working on for seven years, or a script, or a long poem, which has women of colour characters, images and myths, and/or is narrated from a woman of colour perspective? Do you ignore this directive and publish anyway, reassuring yourself that you have researched your material carefully and that it has been written with respect? Do you convince yourself that it is "only fiction," so it doesn't matter? Do you file it away? Rewrite the whole damned thing? Publish it with a disclaimer? You have an increasing commitment to anti-racism yet you are torn; for doesn't a writer's imagination have to be exempt from such dictums and constraints? You wonder, is a directive necessarily a dictate?

The recent struggles within the Women's Press in Toronto and during the various panel presentations at the Third International Feminist Book Fair in Montreal [June 1988] have both provided sites for intense debates among various white women writers and publishers about what I would call our rights to "privilege of imagination." Aside from a receptive response, a frequent reaction to our sister writers' directive has been confused resistance and, occasionally, anger. Beneath this anger, I suspect, is fear. Fear of being gagged yet again; for isn't our hard-won freedom to imagine as feminists our most profound power?

One white woman writer who immediately comes to mind in this debate is Anne Cameron. Her highly regarded book *Daughters of Copper Woman* has been the focus of both accolades and criticism ever since it was published in 1981. In her moving account on the "Lesbian Memory and Creation" Book Fair panel, Anne spoke openly about her writing and relationship to West Coast Native traditions. She described how she had felt compelled to write *Daughters of Copper Woman* to help preserve the fragile oral heritage of her Métis children. She confirmed that she had been "given" the stories with the permission to publish, and that the royalties had been channeled back into the Native community to assist their land claims fight.

While reminding us that no Native women seemed to be writing for publication at that time, she also related the fact that she had recently been asked by some of the Native women writers "to move over." Anne pointed out that there are now indeed a number of very skilled Native women writers who write eloquently about their cultures and perspectives (such as West Coast writers Lee Maracle and Jeannette Armstrong). Anne also spoke of how she had increasingly felt drawn to investigate her own Celtic heritage in her writing, and her pleasure in discovering the resonances between West Coast Native and Celtic spiritual traditions.

In all the conversations I heard and participated in, it is curious to me that it is we white women who insist on our rights to carte "blanche" when it comes to our writing. I never heard this assertion from the women writers of colour. Although we (as women) all experience daily and often devastating oppression, it is the white imagination which has shaped the Western World and it is likely that we (white women) are accustomed to the inherent rights of that white dominion, despite our marginalization. Women of colour simply do not share this illusion.

We say we must have the right to write about women of colour so as to understand their realities. If this is our true motive—why not read *their* books? Include them more in our various public forums and publications? Let's face it: we have not been reading their writing extensively. Yet, as white women, we'll fiercely defend our right to write from their point of view or experience. Are these not the very dynamics we go over and over again with progressive men who seldom read our contemporary writing yet insist they can write from our perspective?

This, of course, brings us smack up against the male-defined literary tradition with its precept that any good writer worth his salt can write about anything. Yes, faintly reminiscent of the omniscience of God. There have been women and men writers who have written very convincing characters who are outside the experience of their daily lives, but there have been many more who have essentially only perpetuated stereotypes and caricatures. This is particularly true of characters from other cultures and races. But we are historically now in a different era with different awareness and concerns. As white feminist writers, our writing is generated out of our experience as white women in a white North American patriarchal world. Fortunately, we bring slants to this experience through our developing feminist analysis (including class), our lesbianism, or our ties with European roots. As well, as women of colour become more and more present and vocal in Canadian and Quebec feminist communities, they are becoming more present in white feminists' writing. Their absence in our work (as characters, cultures and ideas) has been an erasure we can no longer afford.

So, how do we, as white writers and publishers, proceed? I would suggest that when we have characters who are of a different race or culture from ours, we be conscious that we are writing about our perceptions and experiences of them from a white person's point of view. We may need to cue or remind our readers about this in some way. For me, the bottom line is that I don't believe we (as white writers) can write as a narrator or protagonist who is a person of colour. I think it is very perilous to think we can speak authentically from this point of view. As for images and myths, Anne Cameron said, "Their telling is one hundred times more beautiful than mine." Even after all her years of involvement in the Native communities, she says there is much she does not understand about Native culture. I don't mean to say that every time we write about another race or culture we should always emphasize their difference; only that it is a mistake to approach the writing assuming a knowledge we don't have.

One criterion suggested as a guide by Anna Livia during the "Lesbian Memory and Creation" [Book Fair] panel was to do the proper research and "get it right" when writing about a woman of colour's perspective or experience. I said then, and say now, can we really ever "get it right?" Can a heterosexual male ever write about the subtle and erotic intimacies of lesbian lovers and get it right? Would we not challenge him (at least in our minds), question his motives, wonder about voyeurism?

I wonder if we white women are feeling our culture is so stained and depleted that we long to escape it, or at least mitigate it with the newness of another culture. If so, I think we must be vigilant about the possible connection of this urge with colonialism. And can any of us, after reading writers like Toni Morrison or Jeannette Armstrong, really believe we can be in their language as they are in their language? Can we know how to weave the unspoken intricacies and movements of Black or Native relationships? Can we ever realize the associations at play in an Asian or Chicana mind?

We can research the facts and histories (those which have not been erased), but most of this information is locked within the private memories of families or communities. We can imagine or recognize shared personality traits or relationship dynamics. We can relate in some degree to the oppression. Though significant, these aspects are not what a culture or race is constituted from. These are not the artery systems of its survival. The life blood of any race or culture is how its people live in their bodies, how they think, speak and dream.

As white women, when we attempt to write as if we were within another culture or race, we run a very high risk of perpetuating racist stereotypes simply because of the impossibility of our being able to know their wholeness. Historically, our sister writers' cultures and peoples have been taken from in every conceivable way. Is it not time for us to say, not out of guilt but respect, we will honour your words; we stand apart from our White Fathers' oppressive greed; we have finally come to listen, not to take.

Slash / reflection

I was recently nudged into reading Jeannette Armstrong's novel *Slash* by a Native feminist friend who felt that the book was being overlooked by white Canadian feminists because it is narrated from the point of view of a young Native man. She may be right. Many white feminists tend to see the liberation process in independent, woman-focused terms. Perhaps this reflects the fact that white women, as part of the ruling race, have more options than other women for independent action. Because of double oppression, Native women (and other women of colour) do work together with men, for feminism is a tantalizing yet hollow liberation if you continue to experience the crippling constraints of daily racism.

Racism and sexism are strategies of patriarchal thought. In their climb for world domination, white men have excluded not only other races but white women as well. After reading *Slash*, I realized that it is difficult to imagine a piece of white feminist literature creating a white male protagonist who confronts and interrogates himself and his world as wholly as the young man in *Slash* does. I hardly know of any white men who could sustain the necessary courage for this radical (rādix, root) re-visioning. The advantages of privilege are too seductive. As white feminist writers we can only imagine such a male character. This perspective, in fact, would be seen as utopian and, judging from current feminist criticism, not useful or valid. Daydream material.

The urgency and necessity which drives Armstrong's male protagonist knows no true counterpart in white male culture. Yet Native men have often become immobilized by despair. At the Third International Feminist Book Fair in Montreal last June

[1988], Armstrong stated, "In the character of Slash, I was able to . . . have him think at the end the way I want our men to be. I had the power to show them that." The power of words to call up who we can be. Perhaps it's the difference between a culture which is "young" in written language and a culture which is "old" and cynical.

As a white woman, I have no context in which to accurately place this book. Native reviewers, writers and readers know a great deal more about white culture than white people know about Native culture. Within Native culture, the body of written literature is just beginning to take shape.

In her July 1988 review of *Slash* in *Fuse* magazine, West Coast Native writer Lee Maracle remarks, "I am influenced by the European notion that a good book is one that keeps the reader captivated from cover to cover. *Slash* has no such frenzied pace. It is not a European piece of literature. It is Native literature from beginning to end. I read *Slash* and realized that the silence was as much a part of the story as were the words." One of the most profound glimpses of Native culture in the book is when the protagonist, Slash, returns home for a visit. His sister meets him at the bar and tells him that their brother has died. They sit side by side in total silence for several hours. Armstrong's evocation of this vigil is very simple and very moving.

As she follows Slash in his quest for meaning, we follow him through several years of moving back and forth across the North American continent. We watch him become more and more radically politicized as he participates in numerous protests in both the United States and Canada. Periodically, he returns home to be with his family and the land, particularly for the winter dance. As he develops an acute understanding of the political actions which must be taken, he also grows increasingly depressed about the stranglehold of racism, and the conflicting political differences among Indian activists and leaders. His despair sends him deeper and deeper into addiction, and he rages in the streets, "Screw you, you can't suck me in. I'm free. I always will be. I'm like the buffalo man. You'll never own me because I resist. I won't join the stink that you are. I'm a dirty, drunken Indian, probably full of lice and that's how I resist. That's the only thing that makes you look at it and see that I will not be what you are. I refuse. I'll die, a drunken Indian before I become a stinking, fat hog."

After a long binge, face down and confronted with his dying, he reconsiders. Though "ninety percent of my people are dying a slow death," and he "can't stand what is happening to the ones that ain't," Slash listens to an Indian at the detox centre who challenges him: "That's what they want you to think. Them ain't the only choices. There is another way."

The other way is an Indian healing camp. Here he comes to realize what has been missing. Even though he is encouraged by the gains of the Red Power Movement, he has often felt at odds with the leadership, sensing that something was being overlooked in all the anger and political analysis. He experiences a profound healing with a medicine man who passes through the camp. Deeply moved by the power of Indian spiritual ways, he sees that his anger (though justified) isn't enough. He sees that anger by itself eats you up. Armstrong herself comments, "It was more out of anger that I was an Indian, out of resistance, rather than affirmation... I was saying 'I'm not you,' which is different from saying 'I'm me.'"

After his healing, Slash realizes that "being Indian, I could never be a person only to myself. I was part of all the rest of the people, I was responsible to that. Everything I did affected that... Both then and far into the future... they would carry whatever I left them..." He returns home and falls in love with a woman who is political but rooted in Indian ways (though this is not the end of the story). It is a relationship of mutual respect and independence.

As a language-focused writer, one interest I bring to reading is the use of language. In *Slash*, Armstrong weaves back and forth between "standard" English and Indian oral English. I found this constant movement fascinating; it establishes a distinctive narrative voice immediately. Oral syntax is overlaid onto traditional written sentence structure. The result is that the reader experiences written language in a more direct, sometimes unsettling way. "Proper grammar," like "proper manners," shields us from the raw material of what is going on. Black women writers have been circumventing this ethnocentric white patriarchal structuring of language (and consequently thought itself) for years. Walter Ong, in his book *Interfaces of the Word*, describes the results of this disparity: "With writing, the earlier noetic state [primary orality] undergoes a kind of cleavage, separating the knower from the external universe and then from himself." It is interesting to note that young Slash's first separation and alienation from language occurs when he enters the white schooling system with its championing of the written.

One of Armstrong's methods of breaking down the oppressive aspects of written English is her repeated use of grammatically incorrect key pronouns. The one which struck me most was her use of "them" instead of "those." As with "this" and "that," "them" is a more inclusive intimate pronoun: it lessens the sense of objectification. How many times have you heard whites referring to people of other races as *"those* people?" Listen to Slash's beloved Uncle Joe speaking to him when he was a young boy: "Tommy [Slash], you keep it up. You got the spirit in you, that's why them songs bother you so much. Don't deny them. We are Indians, Tommy. Them spirits are crying out to people, the young people, because the land is in pitiful shape and with it, our people." Gloria Anzaldúa writes about the danger of this disparity between speaker and listener in her book *Borderlands/La Frontera*: "In trying to become 'objective,' Western culture made 'objects' of things and people when it distanced itself from them, thereby losing 'touch' with them. This dichotomy is the root of all violence."

In *Slash*, Armstrong creates a seamless complexity through the intricate crisscrossing of different text sensibilities. These include the traditional narrative, the reframing of Indian historical events and the use of oratorical speeches. In an interview with Victoria Freeman (*Fuse*, March/April 1988), Armstrong affirms "that a lot of Native writing is political oratory. That's where much of the motivation for writing comes from—the wellspring of our writing is oral and political."

This is one of the aspects white readers may have the most difficulty with: to white ears oratory can sound like preaching. Cultural associations need to be dislodged in order to read and hear the eloquence and emotion in the oratory which springs from Indian culture. Many Native languages are still in the process of being transcribed into written languages. Consequently, oratory has remained a trusted and essential part of daily life; not a mass media evangelist's or politician's ploy. This is a crucial difference which white readers must bear in mind when reading Indian literature. Native oratory is grounded in the presence and responsibility of both speaker and listener. Western "oratory" is rooted in absence, disassociation and manipulation.

The relationship to history is another important difference. Armstrong has been active in the Okanagan Curriculum Project of B.C. where one emphasis has been the inclusion of personal perspectives along with historical dates and events. History is rooted in the personal. Implicit in this approach is the understanding that there is always more than one historical truth of any given event. In the *Fuse* interview, Armstrong recalls a significant turning point in discussions among the project members about how to create appropriate literature to accompany the historical units: "I had a long discussion with the consultant hired to put the project together. He had brought in some non-Native writers and had a meeting with them about the work of literature for the contemporary unit, and I got really angry at that meeting. I said if we are going to talk about Indian perspective then we should be talking about writing by Indian people... I was not going to see our history bastardized again and some non-Indian paid to do it and getting a book out of it. I got up and walked out... The consultant said, 'If Jeannette wants an Indian writer to write it, she can god-damned well write it herself.' When he spoke to me, I said, 'God-damned right, I'll write it!' I didn't know what commitment I was getting myself into."

Armstrong has previously written poetry and two children's books, but not a novel. In *Slash* she does a remarkable job of presenting the different (often opposing) points of view in the Red Power Movement which not only reflect the centrality of the collective process within the Indian communities, but also the significance of collective process in the development of Slash's thinking—rather a rare phenomenon as far as male protagonists go.

On some levels the story of Slash's quest is a familiar one. Teresa de Lauretis, in her book *Alice Doesn't*, vividly outlines the prototype from which all narrative springs: "Narrative endlessly reconstructs a two-character drama in which the human person creates and recreates *himself* out of an abstract or purely symbolic other—the womb, the earth, the grave, the woman... the drama has the movement of a passage, a crossing, an actively experienced transformation of the human into—man." She maintains that "the hero must be male because the obstacle, whatever its personification, is morphologically female and, indeed, simply the womb." Male as shaper of

72

culture; female as sustainer.

Is *Slash* yet another variation of the theme? Is this analysis even appropriate to apply? Possibly, as it does seem to resonate with Native beliefs in the unity of life (as contrasted to polarization). Within this framework I would say that *Slash* is essentially a classic narrative with a significant shift. Slash does not ultimately conquer/escape "the womb, the earth, the grave, the woman." In part he does, and in part he doesn't: his happiness lies in surrender, not control. He embodies both gender stereotypes of masculine/active and feminine/nurturer. Formally, Armstrong's novel slips outside the skin of traditional narrative through its reframing of the historical, the cultural, the political and the oratorical, and through its reshaping of written English. Lee Maracle considers it to be "the first truly Native novel." I found it to be one of the most courageous *feminist* novels I have read. Both readings are true.

Sources

Gloria Anzaldúa, *Borderlands/La Frontera* (San Francisco: spinsters/aunt lute, 1987).

Jeannette Armstrong, *Slash* (Penticton, B.C.: Theytus Books, 1985). *Order from Theytus Books, P.O. Box 218, Penticton, B.C. Canada V2A 6K3.*

Teresa de Lauretis, *Alice Doesn't* (Bloomington, ID: Indiana University Press, 1984).

Victoria Freeman, "Rights on Paper" (an interview with Jeannette Armstrong), *Fuse*, Toronto, Ont. (March/April 1988).

Lee Maracle, "Fork in the Road" (a review of *Slash*), *Fuse* (July 1988).

Walter J. Ong, *Interfaces of the Word* (Ithaca, NY: Cornell University Press, 1977).

far as the i can see

FICTION: "The action of 'feigning' or inventing imaginary inci-
dents, existences, states of things, etc., whether for the purpose of deception or otherwise... The species of literature
which is concerned with the narration of imaginary events
and the portraiture of imaginary characters."[1]

I sit at my typewriter. I write to you—imaginary reader. As your
eyes lift these words off the page, I become the writer. The
writer you imagine who created this fictionary—as you say
Nicole,[2] "my fictions were reality." And I wonder whose eyes
(I/s) have we been looking into; whom **do** we address? Has our
gender role as women writers been that of immaculate *deception*? Have we like the killdeer cried out and *feigned* a broken
wing to distract the heavy-footed Fathers from our nearby
camouflaged nest? And what of these "realistic" fictions of ourselves which we have read for generations and found barely
recognizable—are they not real to the men who have written
them? Adam naming Eve. The f(r)iction being in their insistence
to import their "real" into ours as superior, in fact, more
authentic. How many times have men argued that women
writers' characters aren't "believable"?

Was it indeed essential to become skilled at feigning
broken wings, until this wave of feminism made us less vulnerable, no longer alone on open pebble plain—our cries now of
anger and delight? We write from the nest and this seems fictitious to the heavy-footed; his bird book (highly regarded for its
accuracy) had theorized (another action of the imaginary)
something entirely different. Even to ourselves we often seem

fictitious and like the "uncivilized" who have never seen their image, do not recognize this figure in the photograph and so stand back and say "who/what is that?" We recognize the chicken, the tree, everything but ourselves—self-portraits an abstraction. Now behind the camera we look at each other, feminine figures of speech, gaze from our own I/s, make ourselves present in this *species* ["specere, to look at"] *of literature*. Seeing as never before—we write new things. Fiction and theory coming together while physics even admits there is no such thing as an objective observer. When we look we change both seer and the seen. Returning the gaze we are often afraid. We have so seldom looked in each other's I/s, so often eavesdropped on our own li(v)es.

Here we are, barely trusting fiction—how can we trust theory (these imaginings historically having reduced us even more)? I remember the great row four of us had (all writers & feminists) over dinner about why was/wasn't theory a patriarchal form—me running to get the dictionary, THEORY: "Greek theoros, spectator, from theasthai, to observe, from thea, a viewing." *Spectator sports*? A room with a *view*? "Theatre" (thea) of the *observe*? "**But** we're writing a **new** kind of theory—fiction/theory." No mind and body split, the text **em**bodying the viewing. Form being the frown line above your left brow, the dimple on your right cheek, the word made flesh, the tissue the text.

Theory having an eye for an I. A seeing ourselves, breaking of the Other's gaze, stepping 3rd, 2nd, 1st person into viewing with our own I/s. Seeing ourselves as primary sources. Speaking subjects who VIEW: "weid-, wisdom, history, story" our own hystery, stories; speak from our own point of view. What intimidates us? Is it fear of what we'll see? Better to remain secondary sources, un(i)dentified (me, you/2 or preferably she, her/3) blind mice, see how they run, they all run after the farmer's wife... blind leading the blind afraid of what we'll find. Invaded enough in every way, why hand over the blueprints too?

Point of view usually she, her/3 and occasionally me as you/2, our I absent in theor ze. Our I our corpus callosum connecting right & left brains the seer & seen self-possessed. Virgins in the original meaning "belonging-to-no-man."[3] A necessity to theorIze in the 1st person, give I witness accounts, if we are to exorcise our wounds, if we are to trust our own gaze. Theoretics/theorethics—hasn't it been another moral of the story, the right point of view? We don't need one more voice of authority defining our literary morals yet this theorizing is not apart from us it comes from **within** our own TEXTS: "Teks-, tissue."

Fiction/theory right (associative, wandering) & left (interpreter, constructive) brains in hemispheric harmony a bilingual conversation of viewer and viewee (I'm of two minds about this), not an either-or situation but 1 & 3 talking so 2 can make sense of her multiplicity—the m( )ther within—this is not dualism but the dialogue of difference. A continual re-viewing of point of view.

We are still uneasy, afraid we'll be misunderstood, criticized for being "too academic," "too intellectual," "rarefied," "patriarchal." Too too. As feminist writers, should our texts be accessible to **all** women? Is this possible? How is this expectation different from universality—a concept that has obliterated class, race, difference of belief **and** us for generations? Are my I/s interchangeable with yours? Do we see I to I? Hasn't the function and appeal of writing always been to see through another's eyes (I/s), glimpse another's point of view?

Stepping into the I of the storm...

I dream of an arsonist setting my writing desk on fire. The dream occurs in my father's father's house. The water is frozen and I can't put it out. The arsonist had believed it held the only copy of my text. The desk self-extinguishes. This seems important to remember.

Going to pieces, this text lacks a COSMOLOGY: "order, cosmetic," this writing called FRAGMENTARY: "to break, from bhreg-." BHREG-: "to vote for (use a broken piece of tile as a ballot), suffrage." Piece of one's mind (I'd like to give you...), voting in a man's wor(l)d—pieces assume a whole we are most often outside of. We live in a state of constant INTERRUPTION: "inter, between + rumpere, to break." Sounds like a mother, sounds like "just a housewife" (unskilled labour), sounds like those of us who are considered "skilled" but still men interrupt what we're saying 98% more of the time than we interrupt them.[4] Our lives chaotic by nature (the World Goddess's womb, Eros born out of)—*between* the *breaks*—we crack the code of Adam's Garden Grammar, our texts interrupting themselves to hear what is being said. Inter-rupt/inner-rupt our bodies the site of other's presence, between the breaks/between the lines, all the voices in our heads—can women fictionalize the feminine?

"You're just imagining things." Yes, we have been all along.

"Only imagination is real!"[5]

78

And the killdeer affect—the killdeer is real, the "broken" wing a real strategy (the foot **is** heavy)—fiction is what we KNOW: "gno-, narrate." Yet fictions we write are unlike fictions men write. FICTION: "fingere, to touch, form, mold. See dheigh-." DHEIGH-: "clay" ladies. I opener: fiction in our hands is to *touch* ourselves/one another, question the *mold*, the *form*, incessantly interrupting the manologue. We view, we touch, this is an eye for an I—fiction/theory (tissue/text) a total body presence.

Sources

1. *The Oxford English Dictionary* (Oxford: Oxford University Press, 1971).

2. Nicole Brossard

3. Nor Hall, *The Moon and the Virgin* (New York: Harper & Row, 1980).

4. Dale Spender, *Man Made Language* (London: Routledge & Kegan Paul, 1980).

5. William Carlos Williams, *Pictures from Breughel and Other Poems* (New York: New Directions, 1962).

induction

showing "our sexts"

women's texts subtext

between
                                    the
                                                                    lines

context pretext *text*:
"in the original language, as opposed to a translation
  or rendering"

                              pre-text
mother tongue:
"a language from which other languages originate"

tonguetext
      "kissing vulva lips
        tongues torque way into vortext
        leave syllables behind

        sound we are sound
        original vocabulary
        language: 'lingua, tongue' "
                              (VI)*

---

*roman numerals indicate quotes from the sequence of poems "open is
      broken."

sentence: "sent, sense, presentiment, scent"

scentext

"the pen gets on the scent" (Virginia Woolf)

syntax

one long sentence
   "homesickness without memory
   yet tongues are not fooled
   tissue 'clairvoyant' "

(XI)

tissue: "teks-, to weave,
   text, context, pretext, tela"

telatext

tela: "a weblike mem-
brane that covers some portion of a bodily organ"

hymen: "to bind, sew,
seam, suture"

"you opened me
[. . .]
an eye with no mind i stood skinless before you"

(I)

we the weavers and the web

webstertext

Mary Daly's "websters"

webster: "a weaver
(Old English webbestre, feminine of webba, or weaver, from
webb, a web)"

between

the

lines

the

warp

is

82

warp: "wer-, inward, verse, version, vertigo, vortex, invert, subvert, universe, prose"

vortext
>"then she was pulled into a whirlpool
>*claim, surrender, sow, manure* flying out
>words her tongue never trusted
>words from another place, old place, vaguely
>remembered"
>>(VIII)

"Her flesh speaks true" (Hélène Cixous)
>>**tissuetext**
>>>*tissue*: "the
substance, structure, or texture of which an animal or plant
body, or any organ of it is composed"
>>>text the tissue   one long
sentence   no period   we are   menses   flow
period: "sed-, to go, exodus"
>>are exodus
>>>"going around in circles"
>>>>(IV)

>>>**exotext**
one long embrace
>"texts of our bodies (tongue come)"
>>>(X)

>>>the route
"the route her tongue took
 the root of the word"
>>(VIII)

>>"root up the word trees
>>in the manure the manuscript"
>>>(VII)

                              tree: "deru, truth" is
in the roots
            etymotext
                        is in the route
                                    erostext
"you claim me with your tongue
  speak my skin's syntax
  know my desire's etymology, *idiom*"
                        (IX)

    intertextuality
                    intersect/uality
                                    intersexuality
"involve,
            revolve,
                        evolve,
                            vulva"
                        (XV)

                            inhertextuality

Sources

Betsy Warland, *open is broken* (Edmonton, Alta.: Longspoon Press, 1984).

84

the failure of the future tense

—no, it's a xerox copy—i mailed the letter days ago!

—well, you didn't make that clear to me. i thought you wanted me to look at it before you sent it—that's why i was pointing out the grammatical error and typo. when you're writing a letter like that you need to be as clear as possible—there's already misunderstanding—why add to it?

—if i had wanted your editorial feedback i would have asked for it! i gave it to you to read for your own information. i thought you'd want to know what was going on. if i want your editorial comments, i ask you for them. i wasn't even expecting you to read it right away.

—well, i think you should always be concerned about grammatical errors and typos. if i were to receive this letter i'd think you didn't care!

—didn't care! i've spent so much time thinking about that letter; writing it over and over in my head. i took so much care in how i said everything. i gave it all the caring i've got! i've reached my limit, given as much as i can, and if she thinks i don't care after all this hurt and all this reaching out to try and heal because i have a typo and a grammatical error—which i don't even agree with you about—then i don't want the friendship. i don't want a friendship with anyone who would base their sense of my caring on that!

—but you're an editor—you know how important grammar is!

—i am very willing to be very careful with other people's work, or with business correspondence, or with final drafts of my manuscripts, but i am not going to pour over personal letters like a business secretary to make certain they're perfect. it's not what is most important in those letters. i'm well aware of your grammatical superiority and i often ask you for copy-editing feedback—but i want it only when i ask for it! i hate it when you've wrenched your whole heart out; put everything into writing something and someone says "yes, it's a good letter but . . . " it's like walking up to a painting and saying "yes, this is a moving painting but is this a smudge and isn't the frame a trifle crooked here?" i find it really offensive. it's a kind of intellectual snobbery i hate!

—it's not intellectual snobbery! i'm not a snob! grammar is important; it can even change your meaning if it's incorrect. i was just trying to be of help.

—listen—all she has to do is read the previous sentence and she'll know exactly what i mean. it's stated right there! i read the bloody letter over for the zillionth time and i just didn't catch it. i refuse to be tyrannized by this!

—well, i won't be tyrannized by you. grammar matters to me!

—and i won't be tyrannized by you. i'm not the one saying you have to be like me!

—yes you are!

—no i'm not. i'm fine with how you are about your own corre-spondence; it's no imposition on me. but i resent your telling me that if you were to receive this letter you would think i didn't care. that's *your* snobbery imposing itself on *me*!

—IT'S NOT SNOBBERY!

—look, i know that you come from a different background about this than i do. i come from a father who had a grade 8 education . . .

—but he was very intelligent.

—of course he was—but he had no choice about getting more education and he spent his whole life being intimidated by this intellectual snobbery [tears running down her face]. he hardly ever wrote a letter because of it. i despise that kind of intimidation: IT IS INTELLECTUAL SNOBBERY! i hate what it did to him. he even turned down a political party offer to run for a major office because of this. i've worked hard at improving my grammar and spelling but i won't have it take over my private voice. my lineage is my father. i'll never forget that. this is my link to him. it's my loyalty to where i've come from.

—i wish we didn't have to fight . . .

—i guess we needed to. i guess we needed to get this clear.

he did write a letter once

when i was thirteen or fourteen and away at Y.W.C.A. camp. my mother was travelling with her sisters to the World's Fair in Seattle. it was a very short letter—maybe seven or eight sentences. he wrote it because my grandmother, his mom, had fallen and broken her hip and was in hospital. he felt i should know. she and i were very close. so were they and i think he was scared. his handwriting was large and curvilinear. very different from my college-educated mother's, which was precise and tight. his sentences were very simple. i felt his loneliness in their construction. i felt his innocence in the written word. it was painful to read that letter. i knew how hard it must have been for him to write it. the words came out in short staccato bursts like someone who was trying to speak after running a very long way.

so how can a feminist

language-focused writer identify with her *father's* use of language? his language of the dominator, the very language that sticks in her throat: erasing her before she even speaks; erasing her *even as* she speaks. but it isn't speaking that she's thinking of (that is another fight, another story)—it's writing. her profession, "vow made on entering a religious order; professio, declaration, confession."

it was her mother who held the dominator's pen; trained in his grammatical boot camp; taught his infantry. her mother. trying to pass muster. the shiny shoes of her letters: the surface the self. how it looked. so much so she revealed little of herself or anything else. the same phrases repeated over and over: like a recipe or a bedtime prayer. names rotating in the slots of "passed away," "beautiful wedding," "visited with," and "fell and broke" or "operation." and when her inner voice emerged— broke the still surface—she quickly retrenched. apologized or attributed it to God (even *then* it was *His* word).

looking at herself she sees

it was in the concentrated honesty of her father's rare handwriting, that she recognized herself. he knew this language mocked him. failed him. found him at fault. he knew he was an outsider. it was always painful—the side of his hand moving across his pristine letterhead; it was always a struggle. every word had to be negotiated. every word had a life of its own. he *felt* the power of the written word. it humbled him. excited him. angered him. each word hung on the edge of what could be said and what could never be said.

cutting re/marks

marker. markher. mark my word. you toe the mark if you want good marks. if you want to make your mark—don't be an easy mark. marked for life. marker—markher! *X* marks the spot. cut it out! chromosome contempt.

dream baby . . . i birthed a baby which they denied me for a day and a half. the hospital would not let me see my baby. i could think of nothing else—my first baby. then i found it. it was a mottled-skinned baby with an opaque umbilical cord an inch wide and over a foot long plastered flat all around its belly. another child, almost a year older, was behind it, attached to it somehow. was this a symbol of the first time i felt impregnated by Daphne a year and a half ago? this child seemed healthy but in the shadow of my infant in/fate. *abnormal "ab-, away + norma, rule, norm."* she had claws instead of fingernails. small cat claws. i went to Daphne's bed (she was in hospital too) and told her about our babies—what did we do? she got up out of bed and we decided to break off the top of the Christmas tree in the hall. we broke it off between the first and second set of tiny branches. a cross castration? *castration: 1) to remove the testicles of; 2) to remove the ovaries of from kes-, to cut, caste, castigate, incest.* cut. incest. i have begun to go there lately, trying to recover/uncover the blank lidded over my childhood memories. my sexuality so evident in photographs until i was 5, stopped dead until i was 31. no feelings, no fantasies, no masturbating. masterbait. provoking words to play with themselves to bait these gods of my repression to speak.

castrate, kes-, to cut. the cutting open of my body for the second time in less than a year. the decision, which i had to make overnight in the hospital: hysterectomy or a "clean up." like—clean up your room. dirt. mess. carelessness. this one about the removal of my ovarian cysts, uterian fibroids, and endometrial tissue. my gynecologist tries to present me with choices. she's aware of my resistances. i'm aware of her preference. there's only one reasonable choice as far as she's concerned. but, she tries: hysterectomy; "clean up"; or go home and do nothing. nothing is not a choice: we agree on this. i could not accept a hysterectomy. would not allow, as H.D. writes, my "other center of consciousness" to be lobotomized. *hysterectomy, hysteria, udero-, uterus, venter, ventriloquism.* the art of *throwing one's voice*, or *speaking from the belly*, so that our words appear to be vocalized by a *mechanical dummy*. dummy—a *practical substitute*. why are there two of me and why this discrepancy? my womb: the "other center of consciousness" or "dummy?"

my ovaries are being eaten up by a dis-ease my mother passed on. she writes "so sorry the genes of your mom cause you to have all these same problems." after the "clean up" all i have left are one-quarter of my right ovary and two-thirds of my left.

incision, to strike, cut/
type, to blow, poke, beat/
write, to tear, scratch/

: my body receiving its text

the implicit violence of the written word
things die, are altered/
issuing forth
from every letter we inscribe
an inaudible little cry . . .

my body struggling with its text. my first book. my mother determined to cut out the first suite of poems. words too graphic too honest about the breakdown of my marriage. she wanted to obliterate them. cut them out before she would let anyone see a copy. my brother arguing with her that people would notice a gap of twenty pages: they would suspect much worse things and how would she explain it. until then she had believed she could cut them out and no one would know. no one would even notice.

"cut it out, Betsy!" only at 37 i begin to say "no."

Cixous urges women to "inscribe" ourselves. mark of the spirit. painted bodies. marked, ritual objects. sacred openings. threshold to altered states. *taboo, exceedingly marked, marked as sacred*. permanent marks on my body. between my breasts. down to my navel. across the top of my mound. my body accepting its text.

crayon held tight in small hand "don't mark on yourself!"

the boundary of my skin has been cut open. *mark, mearc, boundary*. it has known long moments of meaninglessness. eventually, the skin reunites like lips. scarred mouths which need to speak out *my tissue, teks-, text*. i am making these marks. i am marking my words. leaving my marks. my body has forced my *surgery, ghesor-, hand*.

ten months ago, following my gallbladder surgery i wrote: "each day, when Daphne cleans my incision, i cry. cry when she cleans the end of the incision—by my navel. it doesn't hurt—it's just that it makes me feel so vulnerable. does this cut recall the original cut; my mother cut away from me? when she dabs the disinfectant on my wound it trickles down my side and a hor-

93

rible sense of repulsion shudders through me—is it my tissue remembering my blood trickling during surgery? i don't know. those hours in surgery and the recovery room minutely recorded in my tissue but blank in my conscious mind. these sensations lie like landmines buried within my own body."

i didn't want this strange woman to sit so close to us. we had intentionally sought out the vacant corner of the waiting room so that we could touch each other discreetly—hold hands as i waited to be "checked in." *check, ksei-, to rule, Sanskrit, he rules, Old Persian, kingdom, king, shah.* so alien—this kingdom. we huddle in the corner with her sitting two chairs away at a right angle. we hesitate—should we let go of each other? i'm thinking that there are numerous chairs here, she can move to another one if we offend her: it's her choice to be here. Daphne holds on too, so she must have come to a similar conclusion. this woman seems so grey and tight with nervousness and she's so densely clothed. they call her next: "Ballentyne." we relax a bit more as she walks heavily away. when she's asked to put down next of kin, she replies "no one." to come into this kingdom without an officially recognized advocate seems masochistic to me. we decide that i'll put Daphne down as my sister. "Warland." it's begun. "married... children... religion... employer... " i'm shocked to realize how my life cannot be registered in any of these: how utterly outside the formulae i am. within a handful of these questions my life is rendered invisible. my "no" and "none" and stumbling hesitations puzzle my uniformed questioner.

in the elevator. we are being escorted by a bleached-blond, square woman. our escort says "you're going to the same wing." clipped wings; wounded wings. the lone, grey woman stands small and heavy-coated in the corner. says to me "i hope they're not going to do to you what they're going to do to me." her horror falls over me like a net. metal hospital green begins to slowly lift us up like pallbearers lifting a coffin. once you've been strapped in and wheeled flat on your back down these halls and into this cold-sided box—your eyes fixed on its low ceiling—you know how like a coffin it is. maybe that's why people are so uncomfortable in elevators, stare at the floor the ceiling the numbers methodically flashing anything it's not simply an uneasiness created by being in a confined space. with the closing of that door we hear the sound of the last lid coming down.

during the first night we share the same ward. inmates. our beds place us once again in a diagonal position. we don't speak. both enclosed by our beige curtains—the nurse respecting hers, is irritated by mine. both while Daphne is there and after she's gone, the nurse continually pulls back my cloth wall despite the fact i've told her i want it closed. she interprets my need as stubborness: an unwillingness to submit to her authority.

i hear the grey woman talking quietly with her resident doctor. they are discussing her surgery and i hear the word "hyster-ectomy." she seems so alone with her fear. it throbs wordless from her veiled corner. i read Maria Sabina's chants and am calmed. sleep well through the night with my earplugs. enemas and no water or food past midnight. we both have begun our rites. next morning they come for me first. Daphne has managed to get me a private room, so i know i won't be coming back here after my laparoscopy. i've been debating as to how i can let my sister-ward partner know i'm thinking of her. finally, through the curtains i say "good luck, Ballentyne." silence. she's probably surprised i know her name . . . or maybe i've transgressed her privacy . . . then her voice comes back—"thank you."

the next afternoon we walk slowly down the hall to the ward. i've asked the nurses about her and they've all replied that she came through the surgery "fine." i need to get a sense of it myself. the pall of curtains is drawn around her. all that is visible is the *catheter, ye-, to throw, abject, deject, ejaculate, inject, object, reject, subject*, hanging from the foot of her bed filled with blood and urine. we stand wordless in the hall and watch this silent weeping.

have it out
think it out
figure it out
carry it out
keep it out
check it out
cross it out
stake it out
act it out
pass it out
mark it out
hear it out
get it out
block it out
drive it out
cry it out
send it out
mail it out
hang it out
tough it out
tear it out
wait it out
work it out
write it out
put it out
strike it out
stand it out

spell it out
fight it out
yell it out
rule it out
ride it out
reason it out
point it out
push it out
pick it out
hold it out
leave it out
move it out
throw it out
lock it out
lend it out
give it out
live it out
seek it out
cut it out

once we acknowledge it exists
it needs out
which out is up to us

hysteric, Greek hustera, womb. all women by nature are hysterical—so the Greeks concluded and that is that. etymology is
perhaps one of our few true records of the evolution of our beliefs, assumptions, and struggles for power. this history-in-a-
word slowly accumulating, "proving" The Fathers' right to
dominate; enforce their values. contemporary, correct usage
obliterating or condemning those who are not men not white
not monied not heterosexual. Hillman writes "We pass judgement upon people and their souls through this language, group

them, and treat them as if they were these things created by our words... (Remember Freud, attempting to convince his compeers that hysteria existed in men. But hysteria could not exist in me, one scoffed, because hysteria means 'uterus')."

it means what it means.
you can't fool around with langauge.

KEEP OUT

"... only the immature, underdeveloped nervous systems such as found in women, tend toward hysterical reactions."

"Less than one hundred years ago, around the time Freud studied with Charcot in Paris, Richer's treatment of hysteria... was focused on the ovaries. Mechanical devices were invented for compressing them or for packing them in ice."

cool it baby
put it on ice

"Hysterectomy is a major surgical procedure requiring the use of general anesthetic and can have serious complications, including death."

"In Germany, Hagar (1830-1914) and Friedrich (1825-1882) were using more radical methods, including ovarectomy and cauterization of the clitoris. The source of hysteria was still, as in Plato's time, sought in the matrix of the female body, upon which surgical attacks were unleashed."

hysterectomy
his-tear-ectomy
his-to-tear-out-of-me

". . . more than half the women in the United States have their
wombs removed. Imagine that! Every other woman over forty
you pass in the street in the United States has no uterus . . . It's
America's favourite operation."

not to mention breasts
so what we likely have
is over half the population of
women in North America
walking around with no womb and
one or no breasts

we consider this to be normal
in the life of woman
we believe ourselves lucky
to be living in
an era of advanced medicine

cool it
OR (Operating Room)
cut it out
our other center of consciousness
(*hysteris, uterus, ventriloquism*)

i was urged to have a hysterectomy to "control" my endometriosis

HYSTERECTOMY = LOBOTOMY

oh me
oh my
i'm a fool for you baby

i had gallbladder surgery in March 1983. i had gynecological surgery (laparotomy) in January 1984. the same two major surgeries as my mother had, though she is a meat eater and i'm a vegetarian, she a heterosexual and i'm a lesbian, she a mother and i'm not, she living in the country and i'm in the city—my body is still held fiercely. genetic patterns/*tissue, teks-, text* insists on its uninscribed story. the small jar of odd marbles which i discovered in my grandmother's buffet drawer: my child's astonishment when i was told what they were. this story three generations old, perhaps it spans over more—i do not know my great-grandmother's text or her mother's or hers...

we think in images we remember in images images repeat reassert themselves on us again... again...

the lab technician handed me the opalescent container. "Warland, Betsy" was written on it. when i saw the black stone through its milky walls, i felt unnerved. it looked like it was from another planet. egg shaped (2 x 1 1/2 cm), charred black with a greyish-white cap on either end flecked with gold that sparkles when held in the sun. i had this overwhelming urge to throw it in the sea. fear of the unknown. mother's darkness back to

100

mother darkness. i had never seen another gallstone like this. i had never seen anything like this. when i visited my parents that summer, i asked my mom if she still had her stones. she returned with an opalescent container. one charred-black, egg-shaped stone rested on its bottom. twenty-five years ago. twenty-five years later. the image repeats itself until we tell its story until we let it out

two black planets thousands of miles apart yet held within the same orbit

can you see in the dark?
hide-and-seek
"you'll never find me!"

endometriosis, endo, inside + *metrial, uterus.* the image: inside the uterus—

"The uterus is lined with a special type of tissue, the endometrium, which, in reponse to stimulation by the female hormones, swells and thickens each month in preparation for the possibility of pregnancy. If there is no pregnancy, this blood-rich lining is no longer needed. It then breaks down, begins to shed and the menstrual flow starts... with endometriosis, it's a case of the right thing in the wrong place... the endometrial tissue is found growing outside the uterus. It may, for instance, be found on the ovaries or on the peritoneum... even though the endometrial tissue has wound up in some abnormal location, it continues to thicken, break down and shed each month, which, as we shall see, can cause pain and other problems... These areas... may menstruate at first, but as the disease progresses, so much scar tissue is formed that the endometrial tissue is compressed and can no longer menstruate. Thus, there will often be puckered, clawlike areas of endometrial tissue that are no longer active."

"possibility of pregnancy"
"the tissue has wound up in some abnormal location"
abnormal, ab-, away + norma, rule

i thought i would never feel it; believed i would never want it; knew i would never experience it. it never occurred to me that it would happen with a woman. i waited to miss my period. believed in parthenogenesis. "... with endometriosis, it's a case of the right thing in the wrong place." my tissue refusing to "shed." but no second body formed. i only bled inside. bled in hiding. my scarred text. the developing "clawlike areas" my dream-baby's "claws instead of fingers." i read this description of endometriosis only today. the image repeats itself. the body says "write this."

my father and i rushing my mother to hospital. cold-snow, dark winter night. her pain in the back seat. the bucket on the car floor. running out of gas two miles from town (her car—her always pushing people, things to their limit). my dad unable to get anyone to stop. i go out in the bitter-white wind. a young man stops almost immediately (this is what it takes: this wasn't what he expected). her lying in the emergency room. the pain excruciating. she asks for me. she thinks she's dying. we talk. emergency surgery. a burst endometrial ovarian cyst... "chocolate cysts, endometriosis-type, with a very large cyst (5 x 4 cm) on the right ovary and a smaller cyst on the left, with scarring of the adjacent tissue." nineteen years later my report reads "The ovaries were both cystic with prune coloured cysts, the right ovary being approximately two and a quarter times the normal size... the ovarian size was about 4 to 5 cm." she was 56. i am 37. she lost both ovaries. i have portions of both left. i went into surgery prepared, but it was close. when they began to work on my right ovary—the cyst burst.

now i am on the birth control pill to "control" my endometriosis. i am a lesbian. i want a baby from my lover. i almost lost my uterus. i almost lost my *ovaries, awi-, bird*. my mother and i, nineteen years between our surgeries in different countries yet both on the fourth floors. the "gynie" floor—as my nurses say: the diminutives for woman insidious. the *gynecological, gune, woman + -logy* wing. the clipping of...

i am on the birth control pill to control my... control, control. i will find another way.

we think in images. we remember in images. repressed images reassert themselves upon as again and again without our recognition—until we cease to leave them out; cut them out. until we tell the story.

the body says "write this"

we've never met. we're talking on the phone. this stranger's voice says to me "i hate the thought of them cutting me up— invading me like that." not cut but invade. *rape, rep-, to sieze; rapid, surreptitious.* she is feeling what i felt too; what i've heard so many other women speak of. being entered against our wills, even though we yield. "she must have asked for it."

surreptitious, sub, under, secretly + rapere, to seize
anesthetic, an-, without + aisthetos, perceptible

do men feel this way? i hardly know of any men who have had major surgery. my parents seem the classic stereotypes: my mother having gallbladder surgery and a hysterectomy; my father having a heart attack and then a stroke. are there comparative statistics on this? i know women have surgery much more frequently. the forced entry. the flowing of blood. surgery. the breaking in of a virgin. the violent rape. all routine. all very familiar. the way things are.

sitting with my mother over lunch, my father in hospital with a stroke. she telling me all the major and minor surgeries she's had. a long list unravelling over the years, over the dreary food. the dramas of her body. i saw then how she has always believed something is wrong with her: wrong from the beginning. her unexplained blackouts as a child. she has been trying to *diagnose, dia-, apart + gignoskein, to perceive* what is wrong with her her whole life.

who is *perceiving* and who is *apart*? the disassociating of ourselves from our own dis-eases. all the cutting into and cutting out makes no difference. all these sacrificial organ deaths yet no peace comes. there is no such thing as "routine surgery." a part cut out is apart from your body forever. the dead ovary. the dead gallbladder like phantom limbs insist on living again; will not accept unmarked graves. i inscribe them here. they have gone before me and lived my death. they reincarnate on this page.

the stone in me was like myself: a solitary planet. it looks like a planet. i know this stone is the sadness i buried deep ever since i was old enough to know how to do so. the sadness of alienation (*ab-norm*); my spirit always too large; my desires always too intense—disquieting for those i was intimate with. Daphne is the first lover who meets me equally. no happenstance that the stone insisted on leaving: breaking its orbit. that sensation of inadvertently finding evidence of my childknowing: the odd marbles in my grandmother's drawer as she lay in her paralyzed sleep in the next room. my astonishment when i was told what they were. the yellow and brown swirl-coloured marbles. a small jar full of them. enough to fill my 7- or 8-year-old hand. they felt like the sum of words never said. the hardened secrets of her private *melancholy, gall, yellow, gold, gleam, glitter, bright, glad, glow*. the sparkling flecks on the ends of my stone. the stone cinder-black. the flecks. light forced to turn back in on itself?

hospital, ghos-ti-, guest, host, hostile: always on my guard against my host's hostility. only a facial expression away. i am courteous but i keep to myself as much as possible. stripped of almost everything—i am too vulnerable to other people's energies. i am getting ready to "go under" (Persephone and the pomegranate seed); be cut open. all my concentration is required to prepare myself. i need to be ready for anything; at least the possibility of. for anything is possible. that strange saying "if something happens to me . . . " something is always happening to us: this isn't something. this is something else.

the night before my surgery both Daphne and i feel peaceful. the "prep lady" (far from being preppy) comes in to shave my mound. she shaved around my belly button two days ago before my laparoscopy. i'd noticed her nonchalance and humour then. for the first time since i've been here i make an open comment to her when she finishes: "you have a nice spirit." she smiles and says "oh, people aren't always what they seem you know. i've been crying for my husband for the last four years. every night. i just can't seem to stop. he died four years ago. i found him on the floor—he'd been dead for 8 hours—his face against the floor like that. he didn't look happy that way you know. it would have helped if i hadn't come home and found him that way. he was a pharmacist; scottish. the nicest man. we were so happy together. and the cat. he loved that cat. it sat on his lap for hours and he combed its fur just a certain way. the cat wanted to die for weeks after. it would go outside and bury its head in the grass for hours. what do you do? i've cried every night and i can't seem to stop—and then my son. his wife lost her father just a month ago. two weeks before christmas and she was so close to him. he'd had 8 heart attacks, and a half a year ago, open heart surgery for 18 hours... but he died anyway. and she's just like me: can't stop crying. wakes up every morning that way. can hardly get to work. and my son—he's getting tired of it. says 'what am i going to do with her?' i tell him he's gotta be patient with her, she loved her dad so much. but he says she's got to shape up—you can't go on crying forever. i guess it's good i've been alone all those nights. it hurts to be but at least i can cry and not worry. i wonder if i'll ever stop sometimes. do you have 'Faith?' some people say that it helps. i don't know... you know it was such a shock. we were so happy together. he was the nicest man. it was my second marriage and i was so much happier with him you know. my son says we shouldn't go on like this but i know just how she feels—his wife—what are you supposed to do?" it poured out for twenty minutes and then she left with her thick mascara-blue eyelids and lipstick smile. her grief: the air in the room. so thick. our lungs taking short little lurches at it. we didn't want to take it in, breathed as shallow as possible. there was no time left. "visiting hours are over" had been announced several minutes ago and now the flat-toned nun was smoothing out the grey blanket of her evening prayer over the entire hospital. we had to kiss and hold each other quickly before a nurse turned the handle. we had to refind our own peace over the next hours, before we could each fall asleep. in our separate beds. in our separate souls.

the next morning i stood. waited at the guests' lounge window. watched as far as the Burrard Street bridge for Daphne's faded red toyota. coloured metal streaming intently through concrete arteries. i needed to see her out there. moving midst it and toward me. i stood at that fourth floor window and when i saw that red, i vowed not to do this again. i would find another way.

i've stayed away from this "piece" for a few days. stayed away from these feelings; needed a "break" but my sleep-self has called me back. insisted i re-turn. roll over in the night/sharp pain in my *diaphragm, dia-, completely + phrassein, to enclose.* day-self suddenly face to face with night-self, forcing me to acknowledge the dream i just had. sitting up. trying to breathe. ease the pain. Daphne's awake now. rubbing my back. i tell her the dream: "i was dreaming about 'the line'—the long prose-poetry line. my lines—the ones i've been writing lately. all the lines were forming into bars around me/enclosing me/ constructing a cage. i felt so panicky: i didn't have much time—i had to find a way out or i'd be caught behind these bars. trapped for . . . " writing is a constructing of the cage of our own partic-ular/peculiar reality. as i write line-bars gradually build their way down the open page. the dreaded Pan in the woods. the woods at night the tree-trunk dark cage. *trunk, ter-, pass through, overcome*: that moment when we knock the tower of blocks over, when things we've constructed threaten to clone us. self-survival? not destructiveness? we must find our way out. *overcome* our own *trees, deru, truths*. see the trees for the forest. the line must never stop rewrighting itself, as trees recede and re-seed.

Hillman: "By conceiving symptoms as sacrifice, they take on new meanings and receive soul." the symptom not "apart" or a "part" or a "piece:" *symptom, sun-, together + peptein, to fall.* all the pieces falling into place. "Quantum theory thus reveals a basic oneness of the universe. It shows that we cannot decompose the world into independently existing smallest units." and if we are unaware that this is not "routine surgery" but sacrifice—what happens then?

limb. the losing of a limb; not only an arm or leg (is that what it cost you?) but any part of us; any branch any root. limb/limbo.

bitter, to split, bite, bait, fission.

sitting in the waiting room. i recognize the woman sitting across from me; we have a mutual friend in common. after "hello" there's the inevitable "how have you been?" her face becomes in/tense as i tell her that i've recently had surgery. she asks me several questions about it. no deflective "oh" and quickly moving on to another topic. so i ask her if she's ever had surgery. her face gives me the answer before her words: "Yes, several years ago . . . I'll always be bitter about it."

now, when writing this frightens me; when i think perhaps i should be writing "something" else; that maybe i'm simply being self-indulgent—i think of her limbo. i think of the great knot of her face.

being wheeled down to OR. life or . . . entering the state of *or, Middle English, contraction of other*. going to the place Of Other. Daphne walking alongside, holding the chrome side of the Patient Lift (my mother's saying "it gave me such a lift"). lift before the fall.

at the double doors we say goodbye. i look in her eyes: "siempre." tears. blur of swinging doors and i'm wheeled into the Holding Room. this is as alone as it gets. on the brink of . . . the holding of your dear-one's hand—denied. yet, i choose to think of this name as comforting—Holding Room—and feel myself gathered up by a greater, disembodied tenderness. the nurse comes up and asks my name and if i know what type of surgery i am having. she gives me a paper cap for my head, which has a bizarre similarity to a party hat, and asks me if i'm warm enough. she leaves, placing a large clipboard on top of my legs: my storyboard. there are three others lined up parallel to me in the dimly lit room: i pray for each one. i've intentionally not accepted sleeping pills or tranquilizers and seem to be more alert than the others. i wanted the calming to come from within my own body and soul, and it has. we are all going in for different types of surgery (i hear the nurse speaking to each of them). i wonder how Daphne is doing: send her my love. then remember a friend of mine telling of how she was lined up with seven other women, out in a hallway, who were all scheduled for mastectomies. i rehear her indignity at the sense of a conveyor belt lopping off their breasts: "It was like a god-damned parking lot!"

in my mind i talk gently to my ovaries and uterus. with my hand on my abdomen, i prepare my body for the invasion, assuring it, urging it to not resist, struggle against, but rather flow with the presence of these others soon to enter me.

soon my skin will be rendered meaningless.

limbo, in, on + limbu, border.

soon i am going to the place of Other; my consciousness will be taken from me; my memory intercepted. only my tissue will voice where we have been: pain its only syllable. memory a cry or moan.

"Betsy Warland?"

"yes."

"I've come to take you to OR."

"ok."

down the cool hall i think of Daphne. wonder if it isn't harder to wait.

"We're going to room 9."

zenith number: death; enlightenment; fruition . . .

it surprised me the first time—how empty these rooms are. how narrow and cold the surface of the operating table is. two nurses are in the corner counting out loud and in unison the sponges and instruments [two and two makes four; four and four makes eight . . . it never stops] the anesthesiologist comes up, introduces himself and i check with him about the type of anesthesia i've requested. the resident doctor i spoke with yesterday comes up and says "Hi." the anesthesiologist asks one of the nurses to call on the intercom to see if Dr. Simmons is ready for surgery: "Yes, she's on her way." the one nurse attaching the monitor disks on my torso chats about how expensive they've become. except for the huge disk light above me (which is not yet on) and the sound of the nurses counting, i can see no instruments or equipment: no evidence of what's about to happen. only people. later, after my neck had been sore for two days, i found out that a tube had been stuck down my throat. much later, i saw a series of photographs in a book which recorded each stage of the elaborate "draping" the patient before surgery. *drap, der-, to split, peel, flay, derma, epidermis, trap.* the clock on the wall is at three minutes to noon. the anesthesiologist says "Betsy, I'm going to give you your first injection now. It will come through the intravenous and you will feel your eyes rolling back for a few moments. Are you ready?" "Yes." it hits quickly. my eyes have a horrible fluttering sensation, futile fluttering against glass my whole body in a slow

110

motion backflip deep-pit-fall . . . the next thing i know my eyes are opening to a clock on the Recovery Room wall. it's three fifteen.

i immediately scan my body to assess how i am: can tell i've come through surgery all right. a nurse at my side now asks me if i know my name. to her, this question is recovery procedure, to me it is a sign of how radical these past three hours have been. how they've altered me to the core yet all i can say is my name. and i'm grateful i can: it's perhaps the last thread that holds us here. the nurse is now taking my pulse; blood pressure; asking me if i feel ok. my body is shuddering inside. she brings me a warm blanket which feels reassuring. i become aware of the other patients in the room. the drugs are dulling my pain sufficiently and this particular pain is more familiar this time. i remember being so relieved after i woke up from my gallbladder surgery: the pain was not nearly as excruciating as the attacks had been—which no pain killers could relieve. why "killers?" when confronted with something they don't like; feel fearful of— violence seems to always be The Fathers' first instinct and institutionalized response.

as i lie here now, i become more aware that "something" has moved through me; "something" that had total authority over me which altered my body, my spirit . . . everything feels shifted inside. everything seems to be trembling with shock. i lie very still and say a prayer; know i have been held within the circle of light. the anesthetic is the heaviest i've had. it has taken me near enough to the threshold of death, near enough that my soul had begun to protectively move a step before me. like incest—the emotions are all here but the memories are repressed. it is now four o'clock.

"Betsy, we're going to send you back to your room now."

i smile with the thought of seeing Daphne and quietly holding her hand. that connection—my arm, hand to her hand, arm: the umbilical cord birthing me back into this life. she's standing outside my room door when i arrive. smiles. "hi love."

"i've seen her face 2 times now just back from surgery, returned to consciousness, & each time it has seemed so intensely pure to me, spiritual, as if her flesh has somehow lost its materiality—her spirit there so gravely—a grave stillness in her face then as if cleansed of everything but pure being—conscious of just being not of wanting anything, or striving for something, just there and only there—fragile, yes, vulnerable because so self-revealed, but enduring, not strong in the way we usually think of strength (assertive) but in presence of simply continuing even within fragility—feeling very close to her own fate (don't know what other word to use—but it is that sense of shape not her usual identity [personality] but very much hers—where death defines her) & she looks then so completely & purely herself— it is as if i see her again for the first time, fall in love again for the first time, seeing her so clear of everything but her death, toward which she is moving & which also allows her to be who she is."*

---

* quote from an unpublished journal by Daphne Marlatt.

twice i have had surgery. twice i have had my memories of this profound experience "seized." though i heard every word, every sound, though my tissue felt every violation—those hours of broken boundaries within that clean room on that cold-narrow table are a blank space in my conscious mind. an empty screen on my black monitor. not even a prompt.

only a *com(m)a, koptein, to cut*
("what they don't know won't hurt them")
this is the cut that hurts most
this is where the damage is done

,

and this is where the damage is held
condensed on this page
like a tear in limbo

repressed images reassert themselves upon us over and over again until we recognize them; until we cease to leave them out; cut them out.

until we wake up from the com(m)a

the woman who went from doctor to doctor, trying to find a diagnosis for the gnawing pain in her thigh. no relief. no accurate explanation. the pain relentless. finally, in desperation ("it's all in your head") she tried hypnosis (stop smoking after one session?) and there it was. the memory. intact. an intern leaning against her as he observed a surgery which she had undergone. leaning against her. making disparaging remarks about her body. the insult the injury absorbed into her tissue her cells at the point of contact: his arm on her thigh. her pain the words she was denied. after remembering—the pain vanished. she had needed to know her story; she had needed to speak her anger; she had needed to have herself back again. her body, in her own terms. *intact, in-, not + tactus, to touch.*

Louky Bersianik's belief that woman is a victim of amnesia— which is our genderization. our brainwashing so normalized that we are barely aware of it. often our only *tangible, tangibilis, to touch* sign is a gnawing, inexplicable *pain. kwei-, penalty, penal, pine, punish.* the penalty of our gender: the pain we catch a glimpse of in one another's eyes?

the body says write this

i told Daphne about the seagull two days later. i had decided not to tell her—didn't want to worry her. it seemed a private omen: one i was to hold quietly to myself at the time.

at four o'clock, on the day before my surgery, i was lying in bed. no one else was around. suddenly i heard a wailing cry. outside the window i saw a seagull alone on the northeast corner of the hospital roof. it was the most poignant cry: it wailed out four times into the southwest still-grey day. i felt convinced that someone had died and the gull was releasing their spirit skyward. an hour later i heard a baby had died in its birthing "at four o'clock this afternoon." it was the only death i heard of in the nine days i was there (death a taboo). the next morning a gull (that gull?) landed on my window ledge. Daphne and i were astonished as this hadn't happened before. it was so close. looked intent and straight at us as we said "hi!" we were struck by its beauty but i watched in silence. it was here for me, there was no doubt in my mind. though this frightened me, i felt more moved by its purity. it was a magnificent gull with intense, sweet-bronze eyes and sun-white breast. i knew it was waiting for a response from me. i addressed it with my inner voice.

"why are you here?"

"i've come to see if you're ready."

"no, i'm not . . . i have work to do; work which i've committed my spirit to. you are beautiful, i would be honoured to have my spirit released by you, but it's not my time. go away in peace." and it flew away immediately.

for several days after surgery that horrible broken feeling every time you sit, stand, or roll over—your insides avalanching. the fear at first that if you move the wrong way or too much or too fast everything will come undone. the unbrokens' illusion of their bodies' indivisibility. their bodies as shields invulnerable against... *shields, to cut, scalpel.* "let's play Doctor." sugar daddies/surgery daddies. the knife has two edges.

the boundary of my skin has been broken. cut open. it has known long moments of meaninglessness. body parts of hundreds of thousands of us are collected each day and burned to what god?

the skin reunites like two lips. tight lipped: "my lips are sealed." out of these scar-mouths our stories can be told—but this time, we must open them ourselves.

LAPAROTOMY

(Tubal ligation, removal of overy, tuboplasty, ectopic pregnancy, removal of ovarian cyst)

Activities

—no heavy housework for 4-6 weeks
—gradually resume mild exercise, e.g., daily walk. Avoid strenuous excercise for 4 weeks, may swim after 2 weeks
—will require rest period during day
—no intercourse according to the doctor
—may use seat belt

these hospital instructions have been handed out to thousands and thousands of women since 8/78 (the date on the sheet). through all these years they haven't even bothered to notice or change the misspelling of ovary. "overy"—oh very nice of you to come, oh very funny. ask the doctor.

"no intercourse according to the doctor." the gospel according to . . . yes, some women do feel better; freed from all that pain; freed from all that anxiety ("something" growing in there—cancer?). we're told we'll feel much better. just as we're told a hysterectomy doesn't affect our sex life. some women, in fact, enjoy sex more afterwards. but many more women find that their sensual and sexual sensations have been altered; diminished. sometimes dramatically so. they don't tell us this.

what they don't know won't hurt them

"Men with the highest medical qualifications pontificated that the very concept of female orgasm was a fantasy of depraved minds, and beyond belief. Havelock Ellis quotes Acton, a leading English authority of the day, who condemned the suggestion that women have sexual feelings as 'a vile aspersion.' "

i grew up with this:

"what's wrong with Mrs. So & So; is she sick?"

"oh, she just has women's complaints."

complaint, plak-, to strike. a man recently in the paper said he never hit his girlfriend "hard enough to leave marks."

the mastery of making our pain insignificant: invisible.
                              no bruises = no abuse
how we still slink away in shame and silence (Ballentyne). how we wear a fake breast to conceal our loss—what would happen

if every woman were to refuse this camouflage: walk out of her home tomorrow, fling it in the air and go to work; to the post office; to the grocery store; to her exercise class; to a meeting. . . what would happen if the marks were made visible to other women; to men; to children? what would happen if men were brought face to face with their institutionalized medical practices of defeminization? what would happen if all these millions of women could suddenly recognize each other—see the volume and strength of the altered species to which they belong? what would happen? everything would happen. and medicine would be forced to dis-cover other "cures" other "givens" other values.

and if we continue to accept "it" being cut out/covered up? nothing will happen, except what continues to happen in the general routine of mutilating and mutating our bodies.

"The diagnosis of hysteria went through many vicissitudes. . . but 'hysteric' and 'witch' never lost their close association. For instance, in nineteenth-century French psychiatry, an old test for the witch—sticking her with pins and needles—was used in clinical demonstrations of hysteria."

"In his old age, and in a last, strictly psychoanalytic paper, Freud. . . concludes that one reaches 'bedrock,' the place where analysis could be said to end, when the 'repudiation of femininity' in both men and women has been successfully met. In a woman the repudiation of femininity is manifested in her intractable penis envy; in a man this repudiation will not allow him to submit and be passive to other men."

". . . we have no evidence of Freud's ever having analyzed a little girl." so, it seems, that "Freud's fantasy of the little girl's mind becomes a Freudian fantasy in the little girl's mind."

my mother writes, while under the hair dryer at the beauty salon: "I'm sorry that you have some of my experiences of my younger years. I worked like crazy & on projects (really not considering what my body could take & really abusing it). Then when all went very well with what I was accomplishing & the months of work were accomplished—I found it hard to lessen The Pace & when trying to relax, I found I couldn't & health problems & mental problems came. This showed me I must live a more regular & strenuous life." here she rereads what she's written and inserts "not such a" before "strenuous life." my mother, still struggling with her hysteria. trying to convince me (convince herself) that a "regular" life is what she really wanted/wants. then, she writes, "your life will be more secure & gratifying." she says I should find "something that will enhance" my life. something . . .

it was the only time I can remember her being happy, glowing. when she was intensely involved with other women working on church committees, community projects, conferences, radio programmes . . . travelling here and there in cars full of women with purpose. women who had a bit of time to experience their own, independent identity. their own possibilities. their own potential.

but the pressures grew. things mounted up at home. she was gone more and more and things got more and more behind and my brother and i did more and more of the work. it wasn't a workable life for a woman of her time and place. it wasn't a life she could sustain. she could only justifiy her absence as a wife, a mother, and a daughter (to her ailing parents a mile away) for so long and . . . she had to return to living "a more regular life." return to her loneliness and frustration therein.

regular, regularis, containing rules, from regula, ruler. as soon as she wrote "regular" she broke out of it away from it to "strenuous."

strenuous, strenuus, brisk, nimble, vigorously active, energetic, zealous.

my mother's hand moving across the page the first time tells her truth: lets it out. on the second time—covers it back up. *correct, com-, with + regere, straight, rule.* her body said "write this." and her guilt corrected it.

"The hysterical reactions may be seen as desperate attempts to refind body, to incarnate, to find initiation into life."

HYSTERO-RULE

the best science has to offer

the female ovum did not exist until 1827.
science did not confirm the necessity of the egg's conjunction with the sperm until 1875.
conception, until that date, was attributed solely to the sperm.

"It is important to realize how very late in history our scientific understanding of female functioning is."

ovary, awi-, bird, egg

"Before the wind-borne bird became an attribute of goddesses... the Great Mother was represented as all-bird. She bore the egg of creation in her buttocks, which gave her an odd 'steatopygous' look. Her face is beaked and neck elongated birdwise... Many cultures trace their origins to an egg cosmogony at the beginning of time."

in the Tao, the ovaries & uterus are known as the Ovarian Palace, which is the source of Chi and wisdom.

this is not a piece of my mind

this is not a piece

and this is no dummy speaking

i acknowledge my sacrifice

and i embrace my source of power

these are my marks

and this is the writing body

Sources

H.D., *Thought and Vision* (San Francisco: City Lights Books, 1982).

James Hillman, *Inter Views* (New York: Harper & Row, 1983).

James Hillman, *The Myth of Analysis* (New York: Harper Torchbooks, 1978).

Lynda Madaras and Jane Patterson, *Womancare* (New York: Avon, 1981).

122

moving parts

The struggle for the self-determined body is absolutely crucial to all women. Yet, in our "house-bound" minds, we are uncertain about our practical, worldly knowledge. Even though we may be "professionals," our minds' muscles have been trained to push down; against. Our self-recognition is all too frequently rooted in what we are not: "I can't do that"; "I'm not like them"; and "I'll never know what that's like." The I-crises: self more a matter of what we **are not**, as women, than what we **are** and **can be**. It's as if we are caught in a suspended state of labour and our identity is locked at that point in the struggle. If we do "leave home" (figuratively or literally), we are no longer the birther but the birthed. In leaving our father/husband/boyfriend's "house," however, we place ourselves at risk: we live in the world "unprotected." Although we know our notion of security to be false—that our most intimate protector is frequently our violator—we still find the prospect of self-responsibility terrifying.

For lesbians, who are twice defined by our feminine gendered bodies, this struggle is doubly crucial. As our bodies propel us away, inciting a desire which is greater than fear—we take a leap into the unknown, which is the unnamed. With our desire we rename everything: slowly; passionately. And with the gathering of our words we own ourselves: become self-responsible. This takes years. This takes a lifetime.

In the process of becoming a self-named lesbian, every woman must find her way through a myriad of fears. As she does, she becomes less afraid. As she does, **she** becomes the focus of fear within the heterosexual world. Although inevitably mediated (to varying degrees) by patriarchal socialization and economics, she-the-lesbian, has nevertheless, gotten out of hand! For hetero-he, she is no longer manageable. For hetero-she, she is no longer a companion in resentment.

Given this, do lesbian-defined perspectives and imagery speak to or include non-lesbian women?

Considering that language and the canon (as we know them) are central in the maintenance and perpetuation of the values of male-dominant, white culture, where does the lesbian writer, and the lesbian body, stand in relationship to the generic reader?

And, where does the reader stand in relationship to the lesbian writer and the lesbian body?

I have recently re-read my four books with these questions in mind, and will briefly trace the evolution of these three positions by quoting from and reflecting on each of my books. I will also refer to the work of other lesbian poets and theorists associated with the making of my texts. In this self-examination, I will be working on the shifting edge between reading & writing and writer & critic, for the process of self-determination inevitably restructures how we see and go about our work.

My first book, *A Gathering Instinct*, was published in 1981. Among other topics, this text records the shift from the final years of my marriage to my first lesbian relationship.

this circular force

i must tell you
i have held the sun in my arms
i must tell you

i have held the sun in my arms
  have become its burning reflection
                its hot shadow
  have become its definitive horizon
  have become the lids of this burning eye
                        opening like a flower
                        closing like a mouth
  opening wildly like a flower
  closing knowingly as a mouth

i must tell you
i have held the sun in my arms
  have made love to this circular force
          more times than i can remember
  have risen more powerfully than the sun
          more powerfully than the sun itself
          it has shrunk in my shadow
                          shivering

i must tell you
i have held the sun in my arms

Within this poem the lesbian body remains obscured, non-gendered and hidden behind the illusory veil of universality. As the lesbian writer, I associate woman with nature and the mystical. The erotic female writing body is searching for a language which is not forged by the heterosexual, male experience. Typically, I opted for the vocabulary of nature, which has been woman's only rightful turf of representation.

The lesbian writer's position is secret. The poem is written in isolation from the relationship: in solitude, as is often the male poet's tradition. It is from this position of apartness that objectification of the woman lover in the lyric poem can spring.

The poem (and the relationship) is also isolated from the peopled world.

Although the generic reader may identify with the sentiments of the poem, she or he, in fact, is not trusted by the writer. The reader can either transpose the facade of universality onto her/his life (which represents a kind of imperialism), or the reader must attempt to read between the lines: sleuth whose bodies these are.

As a young lesbian writer, I chose this tangentiality for self-protective reasons. At that time, I knew of no poet who was publishing her books as a self-identified lesbian writer in English Canada. The only models were writers such as Adrienne Rich, who published *Twenty-One Love Poems* (1976) well into her writing career, or writers like Pat Parker—*Pit Stop* (1974), Judy Grahn—*edward the dyke* (1971), and Alta—*BURN THIS and Memorize Yourself* (1971), whose books circulated essentially within the American lesbian underground. Olga Broumas's *Beginning With O* (1977)—winner of the Yale Series of Younger Poets competition—was the first book (to my knowledge), by a beginning writer, to be published in the American poetry malestream. In his introduction to *Beginning With O*, Stanley Kunitz writes that because of her "... explicit sexuality and Sapphic orientation, Broumas's poems may be considered outrageous in some quarters... " Somehow I knew that the C.B.C. Literary Competition wasn't about to promote feminist lesbian lyrics in Canada! Nor is it still.

My second book, *open is broken*, was published in 1984. By this time I had fallen deeply in love with another feminist, who was also a writer—Daphne Marlatt. Throughout the first year of our relationship we wrote a series of poems to one another. Although during their writing it had not occurred to us that these poems would be published, our manuscripts were subsequently solicited by a publisher (Longspoon Press). It was then that we began to realize the importance of creating a literary space for books like *open is broken* and *Touch to My Tongue*. In the interim years since *A Gathering Instinct*, I had read, and been deeply provoked by Audre Lorde's *Uses of the Erotic: The Erotic as Power* (1978); Helen Cixous's essay "The Laugh of the Medusa" (which I read in translation in 1981 in *New French Feminisms*), and by an eloquent talk given by Mary Daly on the subject of presence and absence. Still, bringing our love poems "out" into the public was a terrifying thought. But publishing and reading from our books together not only made it possible, but empowering.

III (from the "open is broken" suite)

the leaves witness you unsheathing me
my bud my bud quivering in your
mouth you leaf me (leaf: "peel off")
in front of a window full of green eyes we climb
the green ladder: "clitoris, incline, climax"
on the tip of your tongue you flick
me leaf: "lift" up
to tip tree top
point of all i am to the sky
"roof of the world"
leaves
sink slow into darkening
with my resin on your swollen lips
leave us in our
betrothal: "truth, tree"

In *open is broken* the lesbian body becomes site specific: her body cannot be easily appropriated. Through the use of explicit erotic imagery, the act of lesbian self-naming begins the process of deconstruction of woman as object. Woman's relationship to nature is no longer a passive/receptive or symbolic state but rather an intensely interactive, interconnected state where boundaries blur. The lesbian body, through the the use of word play and etymology, reclaims the existing sexual vocabulary of intimacy. As the body breaks out and opens itself, so too the language opens up—revealing not only the patriarchal codes embedded within our most intimate words, but also revealing how these codes can be broken open: how the language can be inclusive—not exclusive.

My position as the lesbian writer of this text has changed dramatically. Homophobia is confronted directly (in another poem in the book), and as the writer, I affirm my sexuality, which is no longer a source of deception but a source of creativity and power. Here, the lesbian writer chooses to publicly name the terms of her reference: chooses not to remain mute—having them misnamed by the uneasy reviewer or critic. With our books together, objectification is further disrupted by the equal, active presence of both lovers, both lesbian writers. Our two books seem to have been the first of their kind to be published in North America. Suniti Namjoshi and Gillian Hanscombe published a joint collection of their love poems, *Flesh and Paper*, in 1986.

The reader's position has also shifted dramatically. Confronted explicitly by the presence of the lesbian body and the lesbian writer, the reader is admitted openly into the text. The code that the reader is now active in breaking (along with the lesbian writer), is the code of patriarchal language—not the code of an underground deviant language from which most readers automatically disassociate themselves. Subtexts surface and familiar surfaces are turned inside-out.

serpent (w)rite was published in 1987. This book represents my most intensive work in decoding and analyzing language as the bedrock of The Great White Fathers' value system. Dale Spender's *Man Made Language* (1980) was a crucial source of confirmation about the necessity of this language-deconstruction project, as was Nicole Brossard's deconstruction of woman in *These Our Mothers* (published in translation in 1983). Eve and Adam, the original molds of gender indoctrination, are also deconstructed as is the experience of being lost (our post-Garden condition). As the writer, I submerge myself in the experience of being lost: through relentless deconstruction of clichés and decodifying of language; through the interruption by other voices excerpted from a wide variety of material I was reading during the writing; and through the resolution to not go back over and read any of the writing until the text came to its resting point. Consequently, the writing wanders in circles (as one does when one is physically lost), sometimes with recognition of earlier passings but more often with no conscious recognition of the textual landmarks—and so another perspective is laid down in the groove. There are no page numbers, and only in the latter editorial stage did I set the text into eight "turns" which function as indicators of the text's inherent movement (which also evokes women's cyclical orgasmic movement).

from "turn eight"

we are open circle
word without end
a well-come
break down in communication
breg-, suffrage + down, from the hill

over the hill
we are split subject

split, slit, *slot,*
hollow between the breasts
no longer divided against our/selves
we are the subject of two mouths
which now *face, form*
words of our own
prefix and suffix in dialogue
no longer waiting to be heard
no longer eating our hearts out

my word!
eating pussy
         cat got my tongue

we make love in the company of four

two Eves four mouths
refuse, refundere, to pour back
the scent/se of opposition
dis-cover
        language, lingua, tongue
has many sides
dialects,
a variety of languages that with other varieties constitutes a
single language of which no single variety is standard

Although the lesbian body continues to be site-specific in
serpent (w)rite, it is no longer foregrounded. Out of 128 pages,
there are only 8 erotic lesbian passages. In essence, the lesbian
body now becomes the ground from which the writing in
serpent (w)rite is generated. Having established the terms of the
speaking voice in *open is broken* as lesbian, I am centred and
prepared to speak of the world as I know it beyond the lesbian
littoral.

In breaking the greatest taboo of naming myself in *open is broken*, I am now free to address topics (such as war and new technologies) which my status of woman has previously disqualified me from. The search for an integral language is no longer side-tracked by Mother Nature metaphor. It is now situated solidly in the deconstruction and redefining of the very language itself. The lesbian writer's lover relationship, however, still functions essentially in resistance to, and as a retreat from, the world.

In *serpent (w)rite* the reader and the writer are both thrown out of the garden: both are lost; both must be acutely present, for the role of non-participatory observer is no longer viable. Through the use of numerous quotes from disparate sources, as well as meditative white spacing throughout the book, the reader is compelled to enter the text and play an active role in its interpretation. With the emerging concept of dialects, the text embraces any reader whose life and perspective have been marginalized and oppressed.

Double Negative, my most recent book, was written in collaboration with Daphne Marlatt and was published in 1988. The first section of the book, "Double Negative," is a lyric collaborative poem which we wrote during a three-day train ride across the continent of Australia. We were motivated to write this text out of our curiosity to discover how our process of collaborative writing had evolved since we had written the poems in *Touch To My Tongue* and *open is broken*. We were also inspired by the beauty of the Australian desert we were passing through and we felt challenged to re-vision the traditional phallic symbolism of the train. The second section of the book, "Crossing Loop," is comprised of a discussion we had, after we returned to Canada, about the constraints we experienced by staying on the literal and narrative track. In the third section, "Real 2," we broke the lyric and narrative frame by alternately taking a phrase from one another's poetic entries and running away with it—going off track into our own idiosyncratic associative prose reflections.

Perhaps one of the most remarkable things about *Double Negative* thus far is that it has received practically no reviews. Collaborative writing seems to be a radical and unnerving approach for the North American critical mind which champions individualism. It is likely that reviewers' analytical processes have been disturbed by the fact that our individual authorships are not clearly marked in the text. In *Flesh and Paper*, although Namjoshi's and Hanscombe's individual poetry entries are not specified, the reader can identify their individual voices in relation to their differences of race, culture and country.

from "Real 2"

"he says we got to stay on track"

well trained he is we are the only difference being it's his job he profits from it stopped for twenty minutes desert beckoning through conditioned glass he doesn't make the rules—just enforces them dissociative division of labour no one directly responsible for anything fill out a form someone will get back to you form letter replying to form (form is form) she looks out the window what she longs for is the absence of the symbolic to lose track of disappear into this emptiness (his key ring tight around her neck) why this vigilance it's not survival of the fittest (he no dingo she no emu) hand to mouth not their relationship no their hunt is on another plain food for thought word to word fight for defining whose symbolic dominates whose (Adam complex) she wants to migrate she wants to mutate she wants to have no natural predators be nothing looking at nothing thrive in her own absence be out of focus out of range of The Gaze hide out from The Law under assumed names but there's no way out even the desert cannot escape imagin-a-nation of the imaginations of 113 billion who have lived and recorded their mindscapes (real to reel) she reads the "Percentage of those whose memory survives in books and manuscripts, on monuments, or in public records: 6" she calculates possibly 1 per cent represents her gender's memory wonders how woman has even survived the wedge-tailed eagle circles above and the train begins to roll as her hand moves across the page spiral movement (imagin-a-nation) here she can rest here she can play en-counter her anima(l) self pre-sign pre-time touching you i touch kangaroo words forming then shifting desert dunes her desire to untrain herself undermine every prop(er) deafinition she throws the switch on train as phallus ("bound for glory") train as salvation leaves it behind at the crossing loop feels words falling from her like the 50 million skin scales we shed each day breathing stars, moon salt-bush scrub your hand moves across my body (imagin-a-nation) and we settle into this endless motion once again settle into the beginninglessness the endlessness of this page this desert this train this shared desire wholly here with a passion that humbles us what is woman (in her own symbolic)?

In *Double Negative* the lesbian body (although still site-specific) enlarges its symbolism to embrace any woman who is impassioned with her own quest for self-naming and self-determination. Society's negativism toward lesbians is under-stood to be symptomatic of the larger patriarchal attitude which sees woman as negative space. In this text not only does the lesbian body locate itself intensely in the present, but it interacts publicly with "the world," because escape from the patriarchal grid of symbols and values is neither practical nor possible. For even in the desert, which is considered **the** earthly symbol of negative space, the oppressions of race, sex and class are relentlessly carried out; nuclear testing, war games, and archeological thievery thrive.

The lesbian writers' position is now one of writing in the **presence of** and **with** each other as contrasted to writing in the **absence of** and **to** each other. As the private interaction between us (writers/lovers) is documented and embraced, so too is the inherent collaborative process at work in all writing. This acknowledgement calls into question the notion of one authoritative voice (version) crying out in the wilderness. By her existence the lesbian challenges one of the basic concepts of property: she belongs to no man. So too, we-the-lesbian-writers in *Double Negative* defy a basic patriarchal principle of the written word: individual ownership. The collective and collaborative essence of oral communication (the language of the mother and the language of love), is infused into the written word, and the fluvial movement engenders a new in**her**textuality.

The lesbian writers also dismantle another literary formal fence—the division between writer and reader. We-the-writers also become we-the-readers of our own text: we discuss (and document in "Crossing Loop") our reactions (as writers **and** readers) to the first section, and then, we integrate what has resonated with us as readers into a new contexture ("Real 2"). The reader is not isolate and passive but partnered. But— there's the rub! Because love poetry (particularly erotic love poetry) has been essentially the tradition of male poets, the reader's familiar "entrance" to the poem has been "through the eye of the beholder:" the subject; the viewer. With the presence of both lovers, who are speaking, seeing/writing and receiving, the reader's former position is rendered obsolete. The gaze is up for grabs! It is no longer a fixed position of author/ity and control. Because our writers'/lovers' roles are in a continual state of flux and redefinition, the reader's role is also unhinged.

134

No longer standing at the door of voyeurism, the reader must now dive into the unpredictable currents of the text and assume all the varied writers'/lovers' roles. The reader must pass through the initial fear of intrusiveness into the pleasure of inclusiveness. No safe text here. At the outset, often the non-lesbian reader is disoriented by being in the swim of lesbian sense-ability and vision and/or the lesbian **and** non-lesbian reader is disoriented by the flow of the language and form. Here is the irony, for in its defamiliarizations, *Double Negative* is the most faithful and therefore the most open text I have written—for fixed roles can only be dispensed with when we are able to move into a state of shared power and trust.

What this is all about is movement. Our clinging to roles (gender, heterosexual, literary, whatever) is an expression of our fear of the immense mass of energy we are and are in. Recently, I had such an intense experience of this movement that I thought I would explode. When I relaxed into it, I passed beyond motion sickness (fear) into this fierce beauty. As women, we have this body knowledge that we will not explode: that we can move through labour and fear; move through that crucial point in the struggle of pushing against and identification by resistance.

In every reader, there exists a deep-seated longing for the self-named body. Just as a writer's work is often generated out of a sense of absence (of the particulars of **their** story, **their** vision), so too, most readers are driven by **their** sense of absence. Other than practical/information needs, our sense of absence is perhaps our greatest motivation for reading: every reader is in search of **their** self-named body. Not that readers are only attracted to texts which reflect their own lives—quite the contrary; often we find a voice for our absence in "unlikely" places. The writers to whom I am referring are those writers whose life-long quest is to grasp how their particular understandings (of their story, their vision) might be a needed source of revelation and healing. This writing stance is very different from those writers whose work is fueled by the dominator's desire to control and profit from the fate of others who are less privileged.

The lesbian writer is passionate: she has risked, and will risk a great deal to love. She knows she is not alone. She believes that when you never manage to get around to reading or reviewing or teaching her books, you erase essential parts of yourself.

Reading, perhaps more than writing, is an act of faith. Faith in the future. Lesbian writers, along with other marginalized writers, are the voices of the future (which is the present) simply because our voices have been so absent in the past. We are the source of the knowledges which have been repressed, and it is these very repressions which have put the world at such risk.

As women, we have listened and watched for a very long time. And the need for our "quiet" knowledge is greater and more urgent than even **we** can imagine. As a lesbian writer, I call up those parts in you which have been absented by ownership, roles, language and fear—for these are the "perpetrators, perpetrare, to completely perform in the capacity of a father" of my own absence. As women, this is our common ground: it is here that we can listen faithfully to each other: urge one another to speak. It is here that our disassociative isolations fall away. The motion sickness of **re-** is shed; the power of **active** said, and read.

Sources

Alta, *BURN THIS and Memorize Yourself* (Washington, NJ: Times

Change Press, 1971).

Nicole Brossard, *These Our Mothers* (Toronto, Ont.: Coach House Press, Quebec Translations, 1983).

Olga Broumas, *Beginning With O* (New Haven, CT: Yale University Press, 1977).

Judy Grahn, *edward the dyke* (Oakland, CA: The Women's Press Collective, 1971).

Audre Lorde, *Uses of the Erotic: The Erotic as Power* (Brooklyn, NY: Out & Out Books, 1978).

Elaine Marks and Isabelle de Courtivron, *New French Feminisms* (New York: Schocken Books, 1981).

Daphne Marlatt, *Touch to My Tongue* (Edmonton, Alta.: Longspoon Press, 1984).

Daphne Marlatt and Betsy Warland, *Double Negative* (Charlottetown, P.E.I.: gynergy books, 1988).

Suniti Namjoshi and Gillian Hanscombe, *Flesh and Paper* (Charlottetown, P.E.I.: Ragweed Press, 1986).

Pat Parker, *Pit Stop* (Oakland, CA: The Women's Press Collective, 1974).

Adrienne Rich, *Twenty-One Love Poems* (Emeryville, CA: Effie's Press, 1976).

Dale Spender, *Man Made Language* (London: Routledge & Kegan Paul, 1980).

Betsy Warland, *A Gathering Instinct* (Toronto, Ont.: Williams-Wallace, 1981).

Betsy Warland, *open is broken* (Edmonton, Alta.: Longspoon Press, 1984).

Betsy Warland, *serpent (w)rite* (Toronto, Ont.: The Coach House Press, 1987).

difference = invisibility:
the ground of our meeting

in the authorized world as we know it which is the wor(l)d as
The Fathers have told it, Woman is invisible—Woman has only
been recognizable (that is *noticed*) in her **caricatured, car-
ricare, a kind of vehicle** difference; bull shit, (as they say)...
a shit load

as women, it is *in our difference* that we perceive ourselves and
each other: this is the ground of our meeting—what we are not
what we don't want to be what we are (unauthorized) what we
wish we could be what we are afraid of being

it is *in our invisibility* that we perceive ourselves and each
other: difference = invisibility

it is here, at the locus of our greatest injury & distrust, that we
make our trembling attempts to *speak our names hear* one another here on this ground of tears

is it any wonder that we feel such a frightening vulnerability; is
it any wonder that we turn away?

**difference, dis-, apart + ferre, to carry. see bher-, to
carry; also to bear children/bher-: bairn, birth, fertile, suffer, burden, bort "beast of burden"**

difference is a gendered word/difference is a gender

so, as "liberated women," we "celebrate our differences"—at conferences, events, concerts, in publications, or is it salivate our differences (each celebrant leaving with her monosyllabic celibacy intact)?

everyone knows the adage "never trust a woman" or "women never trust each other"; everyone knows that's what's going on behind our nervous smiles

i fear for us, if we cannot come to grips with how deeply threatened we feel when we encounter differences among ourselves—i fear that our names will only be exchanged with those women most like ourselves

i fear we will continue to look to the face of The Fathers for our comfort (which is our forgetting), for in His Gaze we can slip sweetly into the Amnesia of Woman: we will not see *our pain (which are our possibilities)* mirrored back

divide and con-her

as we encounter difference within the feminist communities we are enraged when our disparate names are denied: we are terrified that we will be rendered invisible yet again in the very place we had held out our hope of finally *being seen* this is a well-grounded fear, for as women *our difference has meant our invisibility*: experience has given us little reason to trust it

and yet, if we cannot find other ways to respond to each other than with The Fathers' fear and dismissiveness—we will perpetuate our ghostly roles, police ourselves, never know the **bher-, euphoria** of our own substantiveness

will we persist in embracing our *invisibility as a decoy*, never knowing one another beyond the Fathers' caricatures of Woman, or, can we take our *invisibility as a homeopathic remedy* for our fear, step out from behind our bondwoman smiles: own our creative "burden" as we move our hands across the blank page, the empty canvas of Woman?

Ways & Means

"the breasts refuse" was first presented as "proper deafinitions" at the Canadian League of Poets AGM panel on Women & Language (Vancouver, April 1988). A revised version was presented in the Women and Words panel series (Vancouver, May 1988), and the final version was given at *The 3rd International Feminist Book Fair* (Montreal, June 1988). This theorogram was subsequently published (as "the breasts refuse") in *Trivia*, no. 13, 1988.

"suffixscript" (previously unpublished) was written in 1989 as an addendum to "the breasts refuse". Both of these theorograms will be published in *Writing & Gender* (an anthology of views by Canadian women writers), edited by Libby Scheier, Sarah Sheard & Eleanor Wachtel, Coach House Press, 1990.

"mOther muse" was published in *Trois*, vol. 4, no. 1, automne 1988.

"no central character" will be published in "Recovering the Past: using hypnosis to heal childhood," by Betsy Warland and Cheryl Malmo, in *Healing Voices: Psychotherapy with Women*, edited by Toni Laidlaw and Cheryl Malmo, Jossey-Bass Inc., Publishers, 1990.

"f.) is sure" (previously unpublished) was presented at the Simon Fraser University Women's Studies conference, *Telling It: Women and Language Across Cultures* (Vancouver, November 1988). This theorogram will be published in *Telling It: Women and Language Across Cultures*, edited by Daphne Marlatt, Sky Lee, Lee Maracle, & Betsy Warland, Press Gang Publishers, fall 1990.

"up-ending universality" was published in the anthology *SP/ELLES*, edited by Judith Fitzgerald, Black Moss Press, 1986.

"the white page" was published in *Broadside*, vol. 9, no. 10, August/September 1988.

"*Slash* / reflection" was published in *RFR/DFR*, vol. 18, no. 1, March 1989.

"far as the i can see" appeared in *Tessera*, vol. 3, which was published by *Canadian Fiction Magazine*, no. 57, 1986.

"induction" appeared as one of the introductory theorograms to my book *open is broken*, Longspoon Press, 1984.

"the failure of the future tense" was written in 1988, revised in 1989, and is published here for the first time.

"cutting re/marks" was written in 1984, revised in 1989, and appears here for the first time. An excerpt from "cutting re/marks" will appear in *Tessera*, vol. 8, spring 1990.

"moving parts" (previously unpublished) was first presented as "writing out of the body erotic," at the *From S(censored)X to Sexuality* conference (Vancouver, August 1988). This revised and expanded version was given at the Women's Studies conference, *GENDER and the Construction of Culture and Knowledge* (University of British Columbia, September 1989), and will be published in the selected conference proceedings.

"difference = invisibility: the ground of our meeting" was written in 1989, and is published here for the first time.

About the Author

Betsy Warland has been active in developing the feminist literary community in Canada since 1974. From 1981-1983 she was the initiator and a co-ordinator of *Women and Words/Les femmes et les mots*, a Pan-Canadian bilingual conference of women working with all aspects of the written word. She co-edited *in the feminine*, the proceedings of that conference, was a founder and co-editor (1986-1989) of *(f.)Lip*, a newsletter of feminist innovative writing, and she co-edited *Telling It: Women and Language Across Cultures* (forthcoming in fall 1990 from Press Gang Publishers). She currently lives on Salt Spring Island, British Columbia, and is working on an operatic play and editing a collection of essays by Canadian, Quebec and U.S. lesbian writers.

PRESS GANG PUBLISHERS is a feminist collective committed to publishing works by women who are often made invisible and whose voices go unheard.

A free listing of our books is available from Press Gang Publishers, 603 Powell Street, Vancouver, B.C., V6A 1H2   Canada